KU-444-147

Chestnut Hill
Heart of Gold

Also by Lauren Brooke:

Chestnut Hill
The New Class
Making Strides

The *Heartland* series

Chestnut Hill

Heart of Gold

Lauren Brooke

■SCHOLASTIC

With special thanks to Elisabeth Faith

First published in the US by Scholastic Inc., 2005
This edition published in the UK by Scholastic Ltd, 2006
Scholastic Children's Books
An imprint of Scholastic Ltd
Euston House, 24 Eversholt Street
London, NW1 1DB, UK
Registered office: Westfield Road, Southam, Warwickshire, CV47 0RA
SCHOLASTIC and associated logos are trademarks and or registered
trademarks of Scholastic Inc.

Text copyright © Working Partners, 2005

The right of Lauren Brooke to be identified as the author of this work
has been asserted by her.

10 digit ISBN 0 439 95132 1
13 digit ISBN 978 0439 95132 6

British Library Cataloguing-in-Publication Data.
A CIP catalogue record for this book is available from the British Library

All rights reserved
This book is sold subject to the condition that it shall not, by way of
trade or otherwise, be lent, hired out or otherwise circulated in any form
of binding or cover other than that in which it is published. No part of
this publication may be reproduced, stored in a retrieval system, or
transmitted in any form or by any means (electronic, mechanical,
photocopying, recording or otherwise) without the prior written
permission of Scholastic Limited.

Printed in the UK by CPI Bookmarque, Croydon, CR0 4TD
Papers used by Scholastic Children's Books are made from wood grown
in sustainable forests.

7 9 10 8

This is a work of fiction. Names, characters, places, incidents and
dialogues are products of the author's imagination or are used
fictitiously. Any resemblance to actual people, living or dead, events or
locales is entirely coincidental.

www.scholastic.co.uk/zone

Chapter One

Honey Harper heaved her suitcase onto her bed and looked around the dorm room. "Hey, where is everyone? I can't believe I'm the first one here."

"Do you want me to stay until your roommates arrive? I don't mind," her dad offered.

Honey unzipped her case and lifted back the lid. "I'm all right, thanks," she said, making an effort to actually sound that way as she scooped out an armful of sweaters and T-shirts. She used her foot to gently open the bottom drawer of her dresser and placed the stack inside.

"Really?"

"Honestly." Honey ran her hand over the top sweater to even out a crease and turned around. "I survived the first part of term. I think I can handle a little unpacking."

"I get the message. It's not cool to have your dad in your dorm room!" Her dad laughed, ruffling the top of her head.

"Dad!" Honey protested. She smoothed away the

static so her blonde hair framed her heart-shaped face again.

"Since when did you get too old for your dad to mess up your hair?"

Honey detected the familiar teasing tone.

"Since I was about six years old!" she told him, giving him a gentle shove toward the door. "Go! I'm fine, really."

But when Mr. Harper paused to put his arms around her and give her a hug, Honey squeezed him back like she never wanted to let go. It felt as if everything had changed over the Thanksgiving weekend, and suddenly the thought of being apart from her family until Christmas made Honey want to go straight home.

"I'll call as soon as we get any news," he promised, untangling from her. "Come on, it's not like you to go all wobbly on me!"

Go all wobbly. Honey hadn't heard him use that phrase since he had first announced to the family that they'd be leaving England so he could take a faculty position at a university in the States. That move seemed like such a minor issue now. *I have to get a grip,* she told herself. *The last thing I want is to give Dad a guilt trip.* "I'll keep my phone on," she said with a nod.

Her dad gave her one last hug. "That's my brave girl," he whispered into her hair.

As soon as he had left the room, Honey abandoned her packing. She sank down on her bed and opened her bedside drawer to pull out the album she kept there. A wave of homesickness – for her family, for her old home, for her pony, Rocky – prompted a need to look at pictures of her life before they came to Virginia.

"Hi, Honey, I'm home!"

The door flew open, and Honey shoved her photo album back into the nightstand as her roommate entered.

"Did you have a good holiday? I think Thanksgiving has got to be my favourite. The food is just out of control! I really miss my mom's cooking." Dylan Walsh dropped her bags on her bed before coming over to hug Honey. "But it's sooo great to be back, even though these are going to be the most manic three weeks ever. I'll have to ride Morello day and night to get ready for the league competition." She paused and ran her hands through her shoulder-length red hair. "Well, maybe practising at night isn't such a great idea."

"Definitely not," Honey agreed, knowing full well what her roommate meant. Dylan had been banned from riding for two weeks after she'd tried to take Morello around a course of jumps in the middle of the night. It was all because of a simple game of truth-or-dare, and it had been Dylan and Honey's third roommate, Lynsey, who had proposed the midnight ride. For weeks they didn't know how Dylan had been caught, and it seemed as if she had put the memory of her riding suspension in the past. But just before the Thanksgiving break, they'd overheard Patience Duvall, one of the other girls from Adams House, confess to telling the housemother. Honey knew there hadn't been any time for Dylan to confront Patience before everyone left for the long weekend, and she was certain that Dylan wasn't going to just forgive and forget.

Before they had a chance to discuss the matter of revenge, Lynsey Harrison, the final resident in Room Two, appeared in the doorway, carrying a bunch of leaflets and looking totally stressed.

"What's up with you? You're supposed to have just had a break," Honey reminded her.

Lynsey raised her thinly plucked eyebrows. "Some vacation. I spent the weekend designing leaflets for the school auction. Then I had to come back early to make colour copies in the newspaper office."

She's still putting one hundred and ten per cent into her student council role, Honey thought. Lynsey had thrown herself into organizing the Halloween party to secure votes in the council elections, but now that she was officially a class representative, she seemed just as committed.

"Come on, you can't tell me you didn't get any R and R," Dylan said as she clipped a plaid skirt to a wooden hanger.

"I'll have plenty of time to rest and relax once I'm dead," Lynsey retorted without a trace of humour in her voice.

Honey winced. Before the others noticed her reaction, she snatched up a thick wool sweater and tried pushing it into a drawer that was already crammed with clothes.

"Honey, do you have something against that sweater?" Dylan joked, coming over to give her a hand.

4

"Usually you're like the queen of the well-organized wardrobe."

Honey quickly refolded the argyle vest and put it in the next drawer down.

There was a triple rap at the door. "The girls are back in the house!" Lani cheered as she and Malory burst into the room.

"Lani, people like you should come with a volume control," Lynsey snapped. "Do you want to get us all a detention the first day back?"

Lani shot her a broad smile. "Hey, I missed you, too, Lynsey!"

"We were wondering if you guys wanted to come down to the barn with us," Malory said.

"I'll be down later," Lynsey told them, even though the invite had not been directed at her.

"The barn sounds like a great idea," Honey said, grabbing her jacket and scarf. The temperature had hovered around freezing over the last few days, and even though Honey was sure the barn would be amply heated, she liked to be prepared.

"Excellent," Lani said. "And on the way down, we can catch up on all the news."

"Yeah, like any interesting emails from a certain cute guy?" Dylan raised her eyebrows meaningfully at Malory. "Perhaps one from Saint Kits?"

Malory blushed bright red as she became the focus of every pair of eyes in the room. Caleb, one of the Saint Kits team riders, had asked Malory out on a date at the practice jumping meet just before the holiday break. "Look, what's more important around here — horses or boys?" she joked as she ducked out of the door, her long dark hair bouncing on her shoulders.

"Both!" Lani enthused.

"Well, right now there is a guy I really want to see," Malory confessed.

"Is he dark and handsome with sweet but mischievous eyes?" Dylan asked, putting on her quilted barn coat. She smiled at Lani as they followed Malory out of the room.

"And long legs?" Lani continued. "Maybe four of them?"

"I'm right behind you!" Honey called as she pulled her gloves from her suitcase. She couldn't wait to escape to the stables — and not just so she could hear about whether Caleb had been in touch with Malory. Everything always seemed less complicated around horses.

Honey lifted her head and blew a stream of warm air towards the grey sky. Beside her, Dylan and Lani were reacting in dismay to the news that Malory didn't know if Caleb had tried to contact her over the long weekend. Honey crunched over the russet-coloured fallen leaves and tried to focus on their conversation. *I promised Mum and Dad I'd treat this like a regular school term*, she reminded herself.

"How could you not have checked your email over the holiday?" Lani was shaking her head in astonishment.

6

"My aunt came to stay, and Dad wanted me to hang out with her," Malory explained. "The computer is in his office, which is in the basement. It would have been rude if I'd kept sneaking off to check my email!"

"Lani and I were online for hours over the holiday, but it would have been even more fun if you'd signed on," Dylan told her. "And you didn't make an appearance, either." She nudged Honey.

"Huh?" Honey blinked. "Oh, sorry. I was busy doing family stuff." She slipped her arm though Malory's. "So now you're back at school and have no excuse to avoid checking your mail. How about right after we've seen the horses?"

Malory laughed. "Honey, I thought you were on my side!"

"I know I'm usually the good cop, but I had this sudden urge to join the dark side," Honey teased. It took a little effort to act like everything was normal, but her parents were right. It was a lot easier being back with her friends than she thought it would be.

"So I guess this was your first Thanksgiving, Honey?" Dylan asked. "You don't celebrate it in England, do you?"

"No, we don't," Honey replied evasively. She wasn't about to say that her family hadn't celebrated it this year, either, even though they'd planned to.

"Did you have a good weekend?" Lani pressed, as if she could tell Honey was holding back on them.

"We kept it pretty quiet really," Honey said.

"Don't knock quiet," Dylan warned. "As usual, our

house was invaded by about a hundred relatives. After two days I wanted to break out and come sleep in Morello's stall. The best thing about Thanksgiving is that I realize the perks of not having any brothers or sisters!"

Honey swallowed hard. "I know what you mean about relatives," she said, hoping her voice wasn't shaking. She cast about for some better memories. "Back in England we used to have an open house every Christmas. It was mayhem! At least having to take care of Rocky gave me an excuse to escape twice a day!" Honey had treasured those early mornings, when every blade of grass was covered in crystalline frost. Rocky's hooves had left dark crescents as they cantered around the paddock.

"Welcome back!" Ms Carmichael, Chestnut Hill's Director of Riding, looked up from where she was rinsing out buckets. She turned off the yard tap. "You guys have just broken the record for the fastest arrival back to the stable after a vacation."

"We were all suffering withdrawal symptoms. It was getting pretty gruesome," Dylan told Ms Carmichael, who was also her aunt. "Lani broke out in this disgusting rash." Being the niece of the Director of Riding meant that Dylan didn't have to hold back on her humor around the stable.

Nodding earnestly, Lani began rolling up the sleeve of her coat.

"Enough already. I believe you!" Ms Carmichael held up her gloved hands. "If you really have withdrawal symptoms, I've heard that the best cure is hanging up hay nets."

"Not tacking up and riding?" Dylan hinted.

"You wouldn't want the horses to catch anything from Lani," Ms Carmichael shot back, her blue eyes twinkling. "Kelly and Sarah are taking care of the stable block. I'm sure they'll be glad to hear you guys offered to do the barn. They haven't been able to leave on time in days."

As the girls headed toward the barn, Ms Carmichael called out one more instruction: "I just finished disinfecting stall ten. Could you put down fresh bedding and water, please? We have a new arrival."

"You bought another new pony?" Dylan asked, her eyes lighting up. It was only last month that Ms Carmichael had bought Foxy Lady, Winter Wonderland, and the nervous, beautiful gelding Tybalt, who had quickly become Malory's favourite.

Ms Carmichael smiled. "Not exactly. All will be revealed soon, but right now I really need that stall to be ready."

"We're on it," Dylan promised.

Honey noticed that Malory was anxiously biting her lip as they hurried toward the barn doors. "I hope Ms Carmichael isn't getting another pony because she wants to send Tybalt back," Malory fretted.

Tybalt's future at Chestnut Hill still wasn't one hundred per cent decided. He'd come with some significant emotional baggage that made him tense and bad-tempered around other horses, and a very challenging ride. Despite his issues Malory had believed in him. Honey remembered how Malory had been drawn to him even though he was difficult and closed-off. Malory and Dylan had suggested that Ms Carmichael contact Amy Fleming, who had a gift in dealing with troubled horses. When Amy had taken time out from her work at vet school and Heartland, her sanctuary for troubled horses, Malory was on hand to learn all about using special techniques such as join-up and Bach Flower Remedies. After a lot of patient work, she had been able to use them to reach Tybalt. Honey was convinced Malory would get another chance to prove that Tybalt was right for Chestnut Hill – and good enough for the jumping team.

"You shouldn't worry," Honey said quickly. "Ms Carmichael promised to give you some more time with Tybalt after the way you handled him at the show. She wouldn't go back on her word."

Malory still looked troubled. Honey understood her well enough to recognize there was nothing to say that would comfort her. Malory needed to work out solutions on her own and deal with things privately. Honey knew just how she felt.

"Listen, why don't you go check on Tybalt while we get the stall ready?" Dylan suggested. "I'm sure he's missed you."

"Are you sure you don't mind?" Malory asked. "I don't want to be all melodramatic, but I've missed him, too."

"We're all allowed three drama-queen episodes a

term," Lani reassured her. "It's only fair."

"Yeah, but Lynsey's used up a year's worth already." Dylan laughed as they walked into the barn.

"Thanks, guys. I won't be long!" Malory hurried down to Tybalt's stall.

"I'll go get some straw," Lani offered.

"Ok, I'll see to the hay net," Dylan said, following her.

Which leaves me to get some water. Honey walked down the broad concrete aisle to fetch the bucket from the empty stall. "Hey, Kingfisher." She paused as the pretty bay gelding stuck his head over his door. Honey pulled out a piece of hay that was sticking out of the corner of Kingfisher's mouth before petting his soft muzzle. "Didn't your mum ever tell you not to stuff your mouth when you eat?"

Kingfisher nudged her hand before disappearing back into the stall. Honey walked to stall ten and took the clean bucket to the indoor tap. Some of the other top riding schools had buckets equipped with automatic drinkers, but Ms Carmichael refused to use them because she liked to know exactly how much water the horses were taking in.

When Honey got back to the stall, Lani was already spreading a bale of sweet-smelling straw over the floor, taking care to pile it high around the walls.

"Do you think the new pony will be another show-jumper?" Dylan wheezed as she staggered in with a stuffed hay net.

Honey helped her attach the net to the steel ring in

the wall. "You're not thinking of abandoning Morello?" she queried.

Dylan shook her head. "Not in a million years! Or at least not until I outgrow him." At the sound of footsteps, she glanced over the door and added pointedly, "Morello's a friend, and I can always count on his loyalty, unlike some people."

Patience had stopped just outside the stall, the colour drained from her cheeks. "I didn't realize you guys were here. But I guess I should have known."

Dylan turned away deliberately and started brushing strands of hay off her stable coat. It was clear that Dylan was not going to let Patience forget what she had done, and she wouldn't make the punishment short and sweet. Dylan seemed to savour how the uncomfortable tension lingered.

Honey thought it was weird for Patience to be surprised to see them. If it was unusual for anyone to be in the barn, it was Patience. Even though she was in the basic riding class, she never showed much interest in the horses and showed up only for lessons – or to hang out with Lynsey – which was probably a good thing if Dylan was going to strike an attitude whenever Patience was around.

"Thanks for getting the stable ready, Honey," Patience said, flashing a smile.

"Um, that's OK," Honey said, wondering why Patience was thanking her.

"The trailer just pulled up – are you coming to see her unload?" Lynsey announced as she appeared next to

Patience. "Oh, you got Dylan, Lani, and Honey to get the stall ready for you. Good idea – Dylan never minds getting grimy."

Dylan's eyes narrowed. "So the stall is for Patience? Is she moving in?"

"You mean you don't know?" Lynsey smiled. "Patience's father bought her a horse. She's pure Connemara, and we all know that we need some more well-bred ponies around here."

Honey recognized that Lynsey was taking a deliberate swipe at Morello. Personally, Honey thought the handsome paint was every bit as good as Lynsey's pedigree push-button pony, Bluegrass. *She's just bitter that Morello can hold his own against her purebred.* After all, Dylan and Morello had made the junior jumping team, too. To stop herself from saying something sharp to put Lynsey in her place, Honey bent down and picked up the baling cord that had been around the straw.

"Thanks, Honey," Lani murmured in her ear. "I'm glad you got to that before Dylan did. She might have had other ideas of how to use it."

Honey got Lani's joke, but somehow Dylan didn't look like she was prepared to string anyone up with twine. Curiosity had gotten the best of her.

"Come on." Lynsey tugged at Patience's sleeve. "Your dad asked me to get you."

As soon as their footsteps faded down the aisle, Lani let out a low whistle. "Are you guys having trouble wrapping your head around the idea of Patience having her own horse?"

"Tell me about it!" Dylan made a face. "It must have been advertised as the latest fashion accessory. It's the only explanation."

"So are we going to go take a look?" Honey asked.

Dylan nodded. "Oh, yes. I can't wait to see what this season's colour will be! Is it liver chesnut? Or maybe bay?"

When they walked out into the yard, they found it had become a lot more crowded. A large horse truck had backed through the gates, and two grooms were pulling back the bolts of the ramp. Lynsey and Patience were standing a little way off, watching. Lynsey wore a rather imperious expression, with her hands in her pockets and her blonde hair tucked into the collar of her padded jacket. Beside the truck Ms Carmichael was chatting with a tall, dark-haired man with a deeply tanned face. He wore a long navy coat that screamed "cashmere" over a white shirt and black trousers.

"Ready, Dad?" Patience called as the ramp was brought down.

Honey and Lani exchanged a glance. The man had to be Edward Hunter Duvall, Patience's famous novelist dad. He was quite a celebrity to have in the yard. Unfortunately it would only make Patience more unbearable if they made a big deal about it, which was why everyone seemed to reach an unspoken agreement to keep quiet.

"Do you think they need a hand?" Malory asked.

"I think Lynsey has everything under control," Dylan said darkly.

Lynsey had stepped onto the ramp as soon as it was lowered. "Come on, Patience. You should come say hi after she's travelled all this way," she called before disappearing inside.

Patience walked to the bottom of the ramp and hesitated.

"Go get her," Mr Duvall encouraged.

Before Patience could move, Lynsey appeared at the top of the ramp, leading a beautiful pure grey mare. She was around fourteen-two hands, the maximum height for a pony, with long, slender legs and an exquisitely shaped head. She looked around with her huge dark eyes before lifting her head and sniffing the air.

"You know, I think she's going to be your ticket onto the junior team," Lynsey announced to Patience.

Chapter Two

Honey couldn't help feeling a pang of envy as Patience walked up to meet her new pony. She'd had to sell Rocky when they'd moved from England, and there wasn't a day that went by when she didn't wonder what he was doing and if he was missing her, too.

"I can bring her down," Patience told Lynsey. Patience took the lead rope – Honey noticed a flicker of annoyance cross Lynsey's face as she handed it over – and clicked to the mare before leading her slowly down the ramp.

"She's gorgeous," Malory called, walking over.

Mr Duvall turned and smiled, his teeth flashing white against his tanned skin. "I'm glad you like her. We had an agent scour the top yards for her, and he's really enthusiastic about her breeding. I'm sure Patience will be glad to let all her friends try her out."

Honey blinked. *Um, Patience's friends? I take it she hasn't fessed up to her dad what she did to Dylan last term.*

"I used to ride when I was younger," Mr Duvall said.

"Now that we've moved out to the country, I thought I'd buy a horse for myself, too. Patience will have to give me some expert lessons over vacation to bring me up to speed!"

"I'm not an expert, Dad," Patience protested.

"You will be by the time Ms Carmichael has finished with you," Mr Duvall said, a steely confidence in his dark blue eyes. "And with Minuet being such a good three-day event prospect, we might even build a course back home."

"I did a bit of eventing back in England," Honey put in. It had just been at the local level with her riding school, but she and Rocky had risen to the challenge of combining the precision of dressage with an exciting gallop over cross-country fences.

"You've done eventing before?" Mr Duvall looked pleased. "Hey, Patience, maybe you two should train together! I'm sure Ms Carmichael could lend your friend a horse, even if it's not quite up to Minuet's standard."

Honey didn't dare check out Dylan's reaction to Mr Duvall's comment on the breeding of the horses at Chestnut Hill. Instead, she held out her hand for the mare to sniff. She smiled when the mare blew gently before dipping her head to nuzzle Honey's palm.

"What's her name?" Lani asked.

"Moonlight Minuet," Patience told her. "It's the name of one of the unicorns in Dad's debut novel. The one you're in negotiations with over a movie production, right?"

"Moonlight Minuet," Malory said, not pandering to Patience's obvious mention of her dad's successful career. "It suits her. It's so poetic."

"Hello there, Minnie," Dylan said, rubbing the mare between her eyes.

Honey spotted a flash of irritation on Lynsey's face. *She probably thinks it's unsophisticated to shorten a horse's name like that,* Honey thought. *But I like it.*

"I think we should put her away now. She's getting irritated with so many people fussing around her," Lynsey said, taking the lead rope back from Patience.

But the mare seemed totally unruffled by her strange surroundings. In fact Honey thought she was enjoying all the attention, if her shining eyes and pricked ears were anything to go by.

"Sure, go settle her," Ms Carmichael agreed. "She'll appreciate a rest after her journey."

Lynsey clicked to Minuet and led her toward the barn. Honey loved the way the mare arched her neck and kinked her tail – it was like looking stylish came naturally to her. Connemaras had always been a real favourite of hers. She gave the pretty pony one last glance. *See you tomorrow, Minnie. Patience is lucky to have you.*

The grooms began to unload from the truck several crates of new tack, all in a rich cognac leather. "We've also got her blankets and grooming kit," Mr Duvall explained to Ms Carmichael. He brushed at a stray white hair that had wafted onto his coat "Do you think Patience's friends could help me take everything into the barn?" He smiled apologetically at the girls. "I didn't have time to change after a meeting with my agent."

Honey shot Dylan a warning glance, hoping she wasn't about to point out that "friends" was a loose interpretation of their relationship with Patience. Luckily Dylan seemed rather accommodating.

"No problem," Malory said, grabbing a purple stable sheet and a lunging cavesson.

"Lead the way," said Mr Duvall. He gingerly picked up a plastic box packed full of gleaming new brushes.

"Kelly's cleared a space in the tack room," Ms Carmichael told them. "Make sure Patience knows where everything is."

"So, are you all in the basic riding programme, too?" Mr Duvall asked as he followed them into the barn.

"Actually, we're part of the intermediate programme," Lani answered. "And Malory and Dylan are on the junior jumping team."

"That's fantastic," Mr Duvall enthused. "I'm sure Patience will want to try out for a team now that she has Minuet."

"Minuet seems like the type of horse that would be a benefit on any team," Honey said smoothly before Dylan could say anything about the importance of riding talent as well as a pony's breeding when it came to earning a place on the team.

The tack room was one of Honey's favourite places in the barn. It smelled achingly familiar, even when she was thousands of miles away from her old stable. Two walls were lined with rows of polished saddles and bridles, while another wall had shelves for grooming kits with rails underneath for hanging blankets. Dylan slid Minuet's saddle onto a spare rack while Lani hung the bridle on the hook underneath.

"Thanks for your help, girls," said Mr Duvall. "I'll go find Patience now and see how it's going with Minuet." He flashed another bright smile. "I expect Patience will invite some of you over during the Christmas vacation. We love to have guests at the ranch. It has so much more room than our loft in New York."

He led the way out of the tack room, just in time to miss the disbelieving glances exchanged by Dylan and Lani at the thought of being invited to the Duvalls' for a cozy holiday sleepover! Honey tried not to laugh out loud as she linked her arm through Lani's to walk down the aisle. Patience hadn't actually been too annoying about Minuet's arrival, and Honey believed it could only be a good thing to have another beautiful pony in the yard, especially one as talented as Minuet appeared to be. Honey appreciated seeing well-schooled horses going through their paces, and she couldn't wait to see Minuet being ridden.

One of the greatest parts about being at Chestnut Hill was that there was always something going on – social events, riding lessons, and new ponies arriving in the yard. There was never enough time to stop and dwell on things. And right now, as far as Honey was concerned, that was a very good thing.

Chapter Three

Honey typed in the school password and waited for the email window to open. She'd chosen a station in the corner of the student centre, leaving the others to huddle claustrophobically around Malory's computer. Not being able to wait a moment more, Dylan and Lani had ushered Malory to the student centre right after dinner to find out if Caleb had emailed. Even from the other side of the room, Honey could hear their impatience with how long the computer was taking to log on.

"Give me a BlackBerry anytime." Dylan sighed, tapping the side of the monitor.

"It's doing it on purpose," Lani told her. "Making us wait is the only excitement it gets in a day."

"You guys need to chill! Caleb probably hasn't even sent me an email yet." Malory sounded exasperated; and from the way colour had rushed to her cheeks, she was obviously uncomfortable at being the centre of attention.

Even though part of her wanted to be with her

friends – and to make sure Dylan and Lani didn't intrude too much on Malory's romantic matters – Honey tuned out their conversation as soon as her email account came up. There was one new message in her inbox. Sam. She stared at the sender's name and bit her lip. *Please let everything be OK.*

Taking a deep breath, she clicked on his name and waited for the email to appear. This was much harder than she thought it would be. If only she could somehow divide herself in two, so she could be with Sam and at Chestnut Hill at the same time. *After all, twins are supposed to stick together.*

Honey closed her eyes for a moment and pictured her brother. He had the exact same colouring as her, cornflower-blue eyes and straw-coloured hair that lay sleek and straight. But Sam had preferred his cut short over the past two years so he could spike the front with hair gel. The main difference between their faces used to be that Sam had a smattering of ginger freckles over his nose, but now it was hard to tell they were even related. Now Sam's skin had a pale blue undertone, and he was so thin and frail he looked much older than he was. Honey felt her chest tighten, remembering how Mum and Dad had sat her down in the living room just a few minutes after she had arrived home for the long Thanksgiving weekend to tell her Sam's leukemia had come back. The fact that they'd known for three weeks but had decided to wait until she came home before telling her made it that much worse. Not only did Honey have to deal with the fact that Sam's illness had struck again, she also had to accept the fact that her parents had decided to keep her in the dark, which meant she hadn't been able to be with Sam in the early days when he would have most needed her.

Honey shook herself and began to read the email.

Hey Honey,

Well, thanks to me, our first Thanksgiving will certainly be one to remember! Happy Turkey Day, everybody! At least you'll get a break from me at Christmas – although you're going to have to come to the hospital to open your stocking with me. That's one tradition I'm not letting you out of.

So it was decided. Sam would be going back into the hos–pital for another course of chemotherapy. It had been only a year ago that Honey had been his bone-marrow transplant donor. As she thought of it, her hand strayed instinctively to her hip, where she still had a scar from the extraction. It had been more painful than she could have imagined, but she would have gone through it a hundred times over if it had meant Sam's getting better. It worked the first time. He had gone into remission, but that didn't last. And the transplant could be done only once. Now the doctors would have to find a different approach to fight the cancer that was spreading through Sam's white blood cells.

Honey blinked hard until the screen stopped blurring.

But forget about Christmas. I bet you Nana sends me at least ten baseball caps in the next two weeks. She's more worried about me going bald than I am! Just when I was getting used to having my own hair again ;-)

You were kind of quiet before you went back to school, so I want you to write back and promise you're going to ace the rest of the term. Let me know if Malory and Caleb actually go out. And I want to hear if Dylan gets Patience back for snitching. I'll take any breaking news you've got. Mum and Dad don't tell me anything!

"Hey, Honey, have you finished yet?" Dylan called. "This computer isn't cooperating. It's frozen, and some of us want to know if Caleb Smith is going to ask out Miss Malory O'Neil!" She shot a mock-frustrated look at Malory as if she couldn't figure out why she wasn't excited at the prospect of Caleb emailing her.

Honey decided to write to Sam tomorrow when she had more time. She hit the print button on the screen and quickly logged off as Dylan came over.

"Wow, that's one long email," Dylan commented as Honey went over to the printer.

Honey folded the printout in half and slipped it into her jeans pocket. "Oh you know, some people never know when to shut up!" she said lightly.

"Why'd you print it out?" Lani raised her eyebrows. "Have you got a secret admirer we should know about?"

Honey forced herself to grin. "If I told you, he wouldn't be secret!" She scooted herself onto the study table and dangled her legs in front of her.

"So who's it from?" Dylan persisted as Malory sat down and logged on to the computer.

"No one too exciting," Honey told her. She felt a pang of guilt. Sam was plenty exciting, but she'd never told her friends that she had a twin, which had been even harder than she had anticipated. It was like erasing him from her life when he'd always been the biggest part of it. But she didn't want everyone to feel sorry for her and give her special treatment just because her brother was sick. Her parents had made it very clear that Chestnut Hill was Honey's chance for a fresh start, where she could be herself, without being surrounded by all the associations of illness – the hospitals, nurses, and blood counts. She could concentrate on her education at Chestnut Hill, and her parents could concentrate on Sam. *Mum and Dad expect me to make the most of my opportunities here, and I'm going to prove that I can.*

"She's in!" Lani exclaimed as Malory logged on to her email account.

"You're making it sound like *Mission: Impossible*," Dylan teased, leaning over Malory's shoulder. "Hey, Mal, you've got mail," Dylan trilled like a commercial for high-speed Internet.

"Is it from Caleb?" Lani demanded as she pulled up a chair next to Malory. "What did he say?"

"Give me a chance to read it!" Malory said, flapping her hand at them. "Honestly, Honey, you've got the right idea to keep your emails to yourself! I feel like I'm on a reality show!"

Lani began to read aloud the moment the message appeared on the screen. "'Hi, Mal. Hope you had a good Thanksgiving. Mom cooked a turkey big enough to feed the entire school. I half expected to open my duffel and find a hundred cold turkey sandwiches inside'"

"Aw, cute." Dylan smiled. "A mama's boy."

Lani shushed her and read on. "'Anyway, I was wondering if you were planning to go into town next Saturday. If you are, maybe we could meet up for that coffee we talked about? Let me know. Caleb.'"

"It's a date!" Dylan shrieked, high-fiving Lani before turning and slapping her hand against Honey's.

"He sounds smitten," Honey added, putting her hand to her chest. "'I was wondering if you were planning to go into town next Saturday.'" She quoted, fighting back laughter as Malory gave her the evil eye.

"I would have expected a more mature response from you, Honey," Malory protested, but she couldn't stop smiling.

Lani grinned. "I can't wait to find out what Patience will say. She's going to go ballistic!"

"But she and Caleb aren't dating anymore! He broke up with her at the show. Didn't he?" Malory twisted around in her chair, a worried expression on her face.

"Definitely," Honey reassured her, hoping Malory wasn't going to back out. "He made it clear he didn't want to hang out with anyone who would turn in one of her dorm mates and then lie about it."

"That makes him cute *and* loyal," Dylan said

delightedly. "How can you say no?"

"I'm starting to wonder if you guys are just excited because you think you'll get to come along," Malory pointed out. "You haven't forgotten that we can only go into town in groups of three or more, have you?"

Honey, Dylan, and Lani exchanged glances, doing their best to look innocent.

"You will come with me, won't you?" Malory questioned, her voice strained.

"Of course," Dylan assured her, putting a hand on her shoulder. "We wouldn't miss it. It'll be the high point of the weekend. Oh, young romance!"

Malory rolled her eyes and shook her head. "I don't think it will be very romantic with all of us there – crowded is more like it. But at least the pressure is off. I can truly think of it as coffee with friends, thanks to you guys."

"Coffee with benefits," Lani said, raising her eyebrows.

"Oh, it'll be more than coffee, all right," Dylan said coyly. She turned to Honey. "You did an amazing job turning Mal into Cleopatra for the Halloween party. You should probably do her makeup for her date?–sorry, *coffee* – with Caleb."

"Sure," Honey agreed. "My nana always sends me tons of makeup. I don't know why. She sends me mascara and…" Honey paused. She was about to say that nana sent her makeup and Sam baseball hats. She swallowed. "Lots of mascara and blusher and stuff like that."

27

"That would be great," Malory said, standing up. "I guess I have to try to look as good as Patience."

"Don't underestimate your makeover team," Lani said as they walked out of the student centre. "We can make even you look glamorous!" she teased.

"Oh, you're too kind," Malory retorted good-naturedly.

As they reached the glass doors, there was a gust of cold air from outside as Patience and Lynsey walked in, their cheeks pink from the wind.

"How's Minuet?" Honey asked at once.

"Fine," Lynsey answered, before Patience had a chance to find her voice. "You weren't thinking of going down to see her, were you? I don't think she should be bothered any more today." Without waiting for an answer, she walked off with Patience hurrying to catch up.

"Whoa! Someone is on her high horse again," Lani announced, buttoning up her coat. "They didn't even sit near us for dinner."

"Suits me fine." Dylan shrugged. "In fact, I wouldn't mind if they started eating somewhere else altogether. Like the barn. Except I wouldn't want Patience around to spoil Morello's appetite. He needs his energy for the All Schools event."

Malory winced. "At least you have your priorities straight, Dylan."

"Look, I'm not mad at Patience for turning me in," Dylan said, ducking her head to shield herself from the brisk breeze outside. "I've said again and again that I was stupid to accept Lynsey's dare. What gets to me is that Patience didn't own up to it, and she pretended to be my friend after I had to go to Dr Starling's office. That's disgusting."

Lani shivered dramatically. "Is it me, or has the temperature dropped?"

"Plummeted to below zero," Malory agreed as they headed toward the bright lights of Adams House.

Honey knew they were talking about the mood between Dylan and Patience, but the night was definitely frosty. She couldn't help wondering if Patience had put an extra blanket on Minuet. The pony had looked as if she had a fine coat. "I know Lynsey said we should stay out of the barn, but do you think we should check if Minnie has a thick enough blanket?"

"She'll be fine. Lynsey's got it all under control," Lani reminded her.

I'd definitely be checking on her if Minnie was mine. Honey pictured the mare's beautifully shaped head, and the way Minuet had blown gently on her fingers when she'd said hello. *In fact, I wouldn't want to leave the barn at all!*

The junior lounge in Adams felt deliciously warm after the walk across campus. "Anyone for hot chocolate?" called Lucy Dowdeswell, who was opening a bag of marshmallows.

"Yes please," said Dylan, shrugging off her coat.

"And for me!" Honey added.

"Make that three – no, four," said Lani, with a glance at Malory.

"Sheesh, at this rate I'll have to steal some mugs from the seniors," Lucy joked as she unscrewed the lid of the cocoa jar.

"Hey, guys, we're just starting a game, come join us!" Wei Lin called from the far side of the room, where she and Razina had a Monopoly board set out.

"I used to play this all the time back home," Honey enthused, sitting down on the couch opposite Wei Lin and Razina. "Can I be the Boot?" She picked up the silver playing piece.

"Go right ahead." Razina smiled. She leaned forward to scoop up the dice, her black braids falling forward.

"Where's everyone else?" Wei Lin asked as Dylan, Malory, and Lani squeezed onto the sofas.

"Alex said something about heading over to the library after supper," Lani replied. "The last we saw of Lynsey and Patience, they were going to the student centre."

"I'm still gutted I didn't get to meet Edward Hunter Duvall," Wei Lin sighed. "He's just about my favourite fantasy writer. I can't wait for the next book in his series. The last one was such a cliff-hanger! I mean, how could he leave Ethan Wolfwhisper falling into the bottomless pit of Arythea?"

"Maybe it's not a cliff-hanger. Maybe you're supposed to accept that Ethan Dogchatterer has met his doom," Lani suggested matter-of-factly.

"It's Wolfwhisper. And no one on the fan site thinks that," Wei Lin replied seriously. "You should read some of the ideas people have for how he's going to shirk death this time."

"Roll the dice and take her mind off it. I can't bear hearing another theory on Ethan's hypothetical escape. Really, Wei Lin, you are obsessed!" Razina smiled, handing the dice to Honey.

Honey shook the dice in her hand before sending them scudding across the board. "Five," she announced, picking up the Boot and moving it. The last time she'd played with Sam, she'd ended up in jail a record nine times. No matter how sick he got, Sam was always fiercely competitive. Honey had never worked out if it was because he was the older sibling by six minutes or if it just came naturally. The Boot had always been his favourite game piece, which had caused a memorable argument years ago when Honey had thrown a tantrum after being left with the Iron. Who wanted a boring household appliance? But now that Honey had the Boot for herself, it suddenly wasn't a big deal.

"Here come Lynsey and Patience." Wei Lin waved toward the door. "Come and join us; we just started."

Honey looked from Wei Lin to Razina. They obviously hadn't heard that Patience was the one who had made the call about Dylan.

"No thanks. I promised Tanisha I'd share some of the tracks I downloaded onto my iPod over the holidays," Lynsey said. She headed over to the other group of sofas near the plasma screen TV, where the eighth-graders were watching MTV2. Patience followed her, as usual.

"What's up with them?" Razina asked. "They seem even more exclusive than usual."

"I can't believe we haven't told you guys!" Lani exclaimed. "Dylan found out it was Patience who turned her in! You know, over the whole midnight-ride thing."

Honey watched as Lani's words registered.

"No way!" Wei Lin's eyes widened as she turned to Dylan. "How did you find out?"

"Straight from the horse's mouth, so to speak," Dylan quipped. "I heard Patience owning up to it at the interschool competition. She actually said I deserved it because I had given Lynsey a hard time."

"Oh, give me a break." Razina shook her head. "Patience needs to get a grip. So I guess that news will make life interesting around here for a while."

"Not tonight it's not," Dylan said, passing the dice to Lani. "Tonight all my focus is on Monopoly. Prepare yourself for mass annihilation."

"Ah, a challenge," Lani said, rubbing her hands together. "Would you like to bet the new Camper boots I saw you unpack, or are those just hollow words?"

"I will if you throw in your signed Johnny Damon baseball bat." Dylan grinned.

No way! Honey thought. *She knows Lani would never give up her autographed bat.* Lani loved that thing. She'd had it signed at an All-Star game that her dad had taken her to.

Lani shook her head. "You play mean, Walsh."

"Well, you know, if you can't take the heat and all that." Dylan grinned as Lani threw the dice and picked up a card.

"'Go to Jail.' No way!" Lani crossed her eyes, and Dylan erupted into a gale of laughter.

The girls still hadn't finished their game when it was time for bed. As they walked up the broad, sweeping staircase to their rooms, Honey listened to Malory and Dylan bickering good-naturedly over the hand-in date for a history project.

"I'm telling you it's due on Friday," Dylan said. "Mrs Von Beyer wrote it on the board."

"She wrote Wednesday," Malory said. "Although I can understand you getting them mixed up. They both have a 'day' at the end!"

Dylan pulled out her mobile phone. "Let's call Paris Mackenzie. She lives in Curie, and she can check with Mrs Von Beyer." The history teacher was also the house–mother for underclassmen at Curie House.

Suddenly Honey stopped dead on the stairs. She'd forgotten to turn her mobile phone on after supper! *What if Sam tried to call? Or Mum and Dad?* She grabbed the phonel from her sweater pocket and switched it on, stopping on the landing and bracing herself for a slew of missed calls. Her imagination went into overdrive until she realized no messages had come through. She stuffed the phone back in her pocket. *I can't believe I haven't thought of Sam in the last hour.* She'd been playing a stupid board game while he was lying at home, facing yet another round of chemotherapy.

"Are you all right?" Lani touched her arm.

"I'm fine," Honey told her, but inside she was far

from it. She'd been having such a great time that she'd forgotten all about Sam's illness, how frightened he must be feeling, and how lonely he must be without her there.

How can I be a good twin if I'm not there for him all the time?

Chapter Four

Honey ran her eyes down the list pinned inside the barn doors to see whom she was riding for the intermediate lesson. "Mischief Maker!" She felt a grin tugging at her lips as she read the name of the senior captain's horse.

"You're riding Sara Chappell's horse? No way!" Lani pushed in alongside Honey to take a closer look. "Ms Carmichael must be losing it."

"If and when I ever lose it, I'm glad I can rely on you to warn everyone, Lani." Lani gave a weak smile as Ms Carmichael walked through the open doors. "Sara hasn't come back to school from Thanksgiving yet," the Director of Riding explained. "She has the flu, Mischief Maker needs to keep his fitness level up for the All Schools League, so I'm selecting intermediate and senior riders to exercise him until Sara returns."

"You totally lucked out! Mischief's *so* gorgeous," Malory enthused.

"Yeah, but you still wouldn't swap riding Tybalt," Dylan teased, handing Malory Tybalt's brush bucket.

Ms Carmichael waited for Teresa Harding to lead Snapdragon past before saying to Honey, "Mischief *is* a lovely ride, but he's also used to being ridden by Sara, so you'll have to make sure you give him strong, clear aids. We're concentrating on flatwork today, and I know it's your best discipline, so you should get along just fine."

"Thank you so much!" Honey gasped, feeling a rush of excitement at the prospect of riding the beautiful Thoroughbred. "Can I go get him now?"

Ms Carmichael nodded, and Honey spun around to give Lani a high five. As she ran out of the barn, she heard her friend say, "Did you know, Ms Carmichael, I'm pretty hot at dressage, too? It's one of my lesser-known talents. So if Sara's not back at school by our next lesson. . ."

Honey laughed as she rushed down to the lower yard. Lani was a great rider, but her main talent was for speed rather than the precise discipline of dressage.

The staff and seniors' horses, including Quince, Ms Carmichael's beautiful grey show-jumper, were stabled in the roomy loose boxes.

"Hello, boy." Honey paused briefly outside his door. She pulled a strand of hay out of his long silver forelock before hurrying over to Mischief Maker. She saw his bridle hanging on a hook just outside and took it down.

"Hey, there." Honey pulled back the bolt and stepped inside the stable. Mischief already had his saddle on with a woollen blanket draped over his quarters to keep him warm. Honey offered the bay gelding a horse buscuit before slipping his bridle on. "We're going to get on very well," she told him, taking off the blanket and tightening his girth.

When Honey led him over to the mounting block, he sighed, raising his beautiful bay head and looking across the yard as if he was expecting Sara to appear at any moment. "Sorry, boy. You're stuck with me," Honey apologized, putting her foot into the stirrup and lowering gently onto his back. She'd expected to feel weird riding a horse much taller than she was used to – Mischief was a little over fifteen-two hands high – but was surprised at how quickly she settled into Mischief's long stride.

Honey walked him up the path and across the main yard to the indoor arena. The rest of the class was already warming up by trotting around the ring. Teresa was bringing up the back of the class on Snapdragon. She turned her head and grinned at Honey as they flashed by the door. Honey squeezed Mischief into a trot to follow on behind. She used her legs on every stride, determined to get Mischief working underneath her. She knew he was capable of a beautiful extended trot, never mind a working one. Sara had given a dressage demonstration on him for Homecoming Day, and they'd looked like polished professionals. She heard the clip of his back hoof against his front as he overreached and gave him a gentle tap with her crop. Mischief dropped his head, accepting the bit, and extended his stride so that they seemed to reach the end of the arena in three seconds flat. Honey tried to slow him with a half-halt to avoid bumping into Snapdragon, but Mischief surprised her by halting in a single stride, with his legs squarely beneath him.

Talk about well trained! Noticing Ms Carmichael raise her eyebrows, Honey sat deep and squeezed hard with both legs. Mischief sprang forward in a perfectly collected trot, and Honey concentrated on keeping his pace even, to avoid catching up too quickly with Snapdragon again.

After two circuits of the ring, Ms Carmichael called them into the centre. "We're going to work on your countercanter today," she announced, ignoring Lani's dramatic groan. "The reason we use countercanter is because getting the horse to lead on what we'd normally call the wrong leg on a circle makes him work much harder to balance himself. It's also a great way of getting them to focus on your signals instead of assuming they know what you want." Honey had never tried a countercanter before. It went against a horse's instinct, and it could feel awkward for him. Asking a horse to intentionally go on the wrong lead leg – and maintain it – took a skilled rider.

"Bluegrass already does countercanter," said Lynsey. She leaned forward to flick the gelding's mane so it was all lying on the same side.

"That's great," said Ms Carmichael, the tone of her voice less impressed than Lynsey might have been hoping for. Ms Carmichael turned to the rest of the group and continued. "The best way to get your horse to balance in countercanter is to start off on the correct lead and then, once you come out of the corner, cut across the ring in a shallow loop. As your pony bends back toward the rail, he'll be in countercanter." Her blue eyes danced. "That's the theory, which, as you all know is the easy part. Off you go, one at a time." She waved at Malory to start off.

Malory ran her hand down Tybalt's dark brown neck before shortening her reins.

"No pressure, Tybalt," she murmured.

"Yeah, just think of yourself in a calm, quiet place, Tybalt," Dylan joked.

"He's looking great. There's not a bit of sweat on him," Honey said, trying to reassure Malory. She couldn't blame her for being a little nervous, because Tybalt was still the pony with the most to prove in the yard in terms of his temperament – and Malory was set on his being her pony in the All Schools events.

Malory shot Honey a grateful look as she squeezed the dark gelding forward. They trotted the length of the ring, and when they reached the corner, Malory sat deep into her saddle. Tybalt's trot sped up, and he stuck his nose in the air, resisting the signal to canter. Instead of getting stressed, Malory began posting again and in the next corner gave him another calm, firm signal. *She is such an amazing rider*, Honey thought as Tybalt correctly broke into a canter and listened to Malory even when she pushed him toward the centre, off the regular path. She then rode the gelding firmly back to the outside of the ring in the opposite direction without allowing Tybalt to swap his canter lead.

Honey started clapping along with everyone else. *That has to be another point chalked up for Operation Save Tybalt!*

"Well done, Malory," Ms Carmichael called, looking pleased. She turned to Honey. "Let's see what Mischief will do for you."

"Yeah, go show us how it's all done." Dylan leaned forward to pat Morello's neck. "Are you watching, boy? Look and learn."

"Yeah, it's going to be really hard, what with him being an advanced dressage horse," Lynsey said sarcastically, quiet enough that Ms Carmichael wouldn't hear.

Honey tried to block out Lynsey's barbed comment and concentrate on Mischief. She knew he would have done this a hundred times with Sara, but all Honey had to do was give him a slightly wrong signal, and he'd probably end up doing a dressage movement she'd never heard of. She pushed him into a trot, mentally running through the countercanter aids Ms Carmichael had given them.

Mischief broke into a canter on the right lead, and Honey guided him off the track and circled to the left.She could feel Mischief's hind legs working powerfully and knew without glancing down that he was pulling off a fantastic countercanter. It didn't feel at all uncomfortable or unbalanced, even though he was now leading with his outside leg. *We did it!*

"Perfect," Ms Carmichael called before sending Dylan down the arena on Morello. Honey pulled up alongside Malory, who flashed her a grin.

"It feels amazing when you get them to do something that they think is all wrong, huh?" Malory asked.

"It's a power trip." Honey laughed, patting Mischief's neck.

Dylan trotted up and pulled a face. "Morello just doesn't get countercanter. He thinks I'm completely crazy and ignores me. Did you see the flying change he did when we came back to the rail! He's annoyed now because I haven't thanked him for bailing us out."

"Dylan, you need to be stronger with your legs so Morello knows you're in charge," Ms Carmichael called over.

"Do you hear that?" Dylan leaned forward to speak into Morello's ear. "I'm the boss, apparently!"

Morello snorted and shook his head. Dylan grinned. "Dumb horse."

"He's never going to believe you if you insult him," Honey teased. "Besides, he knows you're smitten."

Ms Carmichael came into the centre of the ring as Lynsey finished the lesson with a demonstration of how countercanter should be performed – though Honey knew Bluegrass wasn't any more polished than Mischief. "Really good, everybody. Next lesson we can move on to flying changes, which Dylan and Morello should find much easier!" Ms Carmichael looked at her watch. "Walk them on a loose rein to cool them down before you untack them, please. We need to finish a little early today since I have a meeting about something that could be very exciting for our riding programme."

"What is it?" Dylan asked.

"Allbrights cheated at the interschools competition, and they have to forfeit the season?" Lani shot out.

Ms Carmichael held her hand up. "That's enough, Lani. The last thing I want is for rumours like that to get around the entire school."

"And the other schools. We have contacts," Lani warned without a moment's hesitation.

"Well, before you send out the informants, I'd better set the record straight. I'm seeing Dr Starling about the possibility of constructing a cross-country course on campus," Ms Carmichael told them.

Lani let out a wolf whistle, making Bluegrass snatch at his bridle and swerve sideways.

"Watch it!" Lynsey snapped.

"That would be awesome!". said Dylan. "I bet Morello would be brilliant."

"Would that be because there aren't so many tight corners on cross-country courses?" Malory teased. It was common knowledge that Morello's pet peeve was jumping out of a close corner.

"It's in the early stages of discussion. We need permission to even draw up the plans, so no trekking into the woods to do off-road jumping to prove a point!" Ms Carmichael called out. "I'll let you know if we get approval. So quiet down and see to your horses, please."

The girls walked their ponies a couple of times

around the arena, and then Honey left the others to take Mischief to the back stable block. She groaned when she dismounted. Her legs were going to ache like crazy with all the extra work she'd put in. She rubbed Mischief down and checked that his hay net was full before buckling on his blanket. "Thanks, boy," she whispered, stretching up to run her hand along his mane. "And don't worry, Sara will be back soon. I promise." At the sound of his owner's name, Mischief's ears flicked forward. Honey couldn't resist giving him one more hug before heading back up to the main yard. She loved horses that made a special connection with people, like Tybalt had with Malory. As much as she loved all the ponies at Chestnut Hill, that feeling of true friendship was what she missed most when she thought of Rocky. She hadn't had any really close friends back in England. Apart from spending most of her spare time with her pony, she'd always had Sam to confide in. He'd been the only best friend she'd ever needed.

Malory, Lani, and Dylan were waiting for her at the top of the path. "We're going to watch the end of the basic lesson. Do you want to come?" Malory called. "We want to see Minuet in action."

"Great idea." Honey knew she'd enjoy seeing how Patience got on with her new pony.

"So, after riding Mischief do you think you can bear going back to riding anything less than an advanced dressage horse?" Lani teased as they walked down to the outdoor ring.

43

Honey grinned. "What makes you think that it isn't Mischief who won't be able to bear anyone but me now?"

"In your dreams, Harper," Lani retorted. "Sara better get back soon to put your ego in check."

Honey gave her a gentle push, but she couldn't help wishing she had a favourite pony at Chestnut Hill. Lani always favoured Colorado; Dylan had Morello; and Malory, Tybalt; but Honey hadn't formed a special partnership with any horse since Rocky. *Maybe I'm a one-pony girl.* She suddenly felt a pang of homesickness. Too much had changed in the last year. Sam had fallen sick; she'd had to leave Rocky in England; and she'd stopped living with her family to go away to school. If she hadn't made such great friends at Chestnut Hill, she didn't think she could have coped this far.

"Lynsey's here, too," Dylan announced, nodding toward the fence. Lynsey didn't seem to hear them coming. She was completely absorbed in watching the basic class trot over a row of poles, ending in a low fence.

"Use your legs!" Lynsey seemed to hiss as Patience rode by.

Minuet was sandwiched between Kingfisher and Nutmeg. Even though Patience was riding too close to Kingfisher, and Nutmeg's rider was crowding in from behind, Honey noticed the grey mare was still trotting calmly, without being unnerved by having the other ponies so near.

"What's with the traffic jam over there?" Roger

Musgrave shouted in his clipped English accent. "Fall back and leave one pony's space between you!" The trainer tapped his whip impatiently against his long, polished boots.

Yikes, I hope the others don't think all English instructors are like that, Honey thought. A picture of Lily, the equestrian student at her local stable back home, flashed into Honey's mind. She wondered what Mr Musgrave would make of Lily's bright pink hair and steady uniform of concert T-shirts; she might not have looked like a regular riding instructor, but she'd been an inspiration to Honey. The horses never seemed to notice her nose rings or her Day-Glo hair, and Lily always had great advice for getting just a little extra out of Rocky and the other mounts.

"And sit deep as you approach the fence," Mr Musgrave continued from the centre of the arena. "Really you should all be able to ride without stirrups without bouncing up and down like you're on pogo sticks."

Honey tried to hide a grin. The truth was most of the riders were moving naturally with their ponies' rhythm, even though their stirrups were crossed in front of them. Only Patience seemed to be uncomfortable; Honey noticed her grab the pommel to pull herself straight in the saddle every few strides.

Minuet turned down the long side of the ring and trotted over the poles in a gorgeous floating movement before lifting her legs and sailing gracefully over the crossbar. As they landed Patience grabbed a handful of mane, dropping her contact with the mare's mouth.

"Pick up your reins!" Lynsey cupped her hands to shout as Minuet broke into a canter and Patience lurched in the saddle.

"Oh boy, the dictator isn't going to like that," Lani whispered, glancing at the instructor.

"Halt!" Mr Musgrave called, striding toward them.

Minuet's ears flicked backward as she neared the end of the arena, but she continued cantering, and Patience continued to lose control as she slid forward in the saddle.

"She's about to eat dirt," Lani predicted as Patience slipped perilously toward the sand.

But Minuet obviously realized her rider was in trouble, and instead of taking advantage and ducking sideways, she slowed to an even trot and then came to a halt.

Mr Musgrave took hold of Minuet's bridle while Patience pulled herself back into the saddle. "Are you all right?" he asked, looking at Patience from under the brim of his flat tweed cap.

Patience nodded, fumbling for her reins. She shot a glance at Lynsey, her face going bright red. *It can't be easy riding Minnie for the first time in front of us all*, Honey thought sympathetically. She knew her own first few outings on Rocky had been, well, rocky!

"Maybe if she tried concentrating on her horse instead of what Lynsey thinks of her, she'd have a better chance of staying on," Dylan commented.

"Try again, and this time let yourself relax into her

stride," the coach told Patience before walking back into the middle of the schooling ring. He pulled his cap down further over his short grey hair. "Class, carry on. With no further comments from the sidelines, please." He glanced pointedly at Lynsey.

Minuet picked up a spritely trot as soon as Patience gave her a nudge.

"Wow, that's one steady pony," Malory said, leaning her arms on the fence post. "She seems so sweet and willing."

Lani nodded. "Connemaras are supposed to be really easygoing. They are brave yet intelligent."

"It's probably because they come from sturdy Irish stock," Dylan offered. "They are bred to be up for anything."

Honey ran her eyes over the grey mare again, noting her strong, sloping shoulder and deep, compact body. She remembered reading about a Connemara pony that had won at Hickstead, the most prestigious outdoor show-jumping event in the UK. She told the others about him. "Stroller, I think his name was. He was only fourteen-two, but he beat off all the full-size horses."

"Yeah. Wasn't he the only true pony ever to compete in the Olympics? Who knows? Mr Duvall's competition plans for Patience might still come true," Dylan said, her lips twitching with a grin since she clearly didn't believe what she was saying.

Patience steered Minuet to follow Kingfisher over the poles once more, but she still looked tense and didn't relax into her pony's smooth stride. Minuet popped over the small jump and stayed in a slow trot afterward, as though she remembered the trouble Patience had with the canter the last time. Although Patience didn't have the balance to urge Minuet into a canter, she did manage to post evenly down the length of the ring.

"Better, but you're still not using your legs enough," Lynsey prompted as her friend rode past her.

Honey couldn't help feeling a jolt of sympathy for Patience. *I guess I didn't realize how lucky I was being able to make mistakes on Rocky without any pressure.* Honey had pretty much learned how to ride on her own. Sam hadn't taken any interest in horses; and when her parents had bought the sturdy New Forest pony for Honey, they had made a big deal about how this was a hobby of her own. Honey had always struggled to keep up with Sam, particularly in athletics. If Sam had taken up riding, he probably would have been a natural, just as he was at everything else! But Sam was happy devoting himself to playing rugby while Honey spent as much time as possible with her gorgeous bay pony. Their parents had always encouraged them to have different hobbies, but right now Honey wondered if all those hours apart had been worth it.

Mr Musgrave glanced at his watch. "That's it for today. Take back your stirrups."

"I'll catch up with you in a minute," Lynsey called to Patience. She turned to Honey and the others, who were still standing by the fence. "Did you notice how well behaved Minuet was?" she asked, looking wide-eyed at Malory. "It's so good to have a *reliable* pony, don't you think? I told Patience, if she works hard, she might make the team at the next tryouts. We need a horse that's got some good breeding." She aimed this final insult at Dylan, smiling the whole time.

Dylan's green eyes darkened, and Honey braced herself for a biting retort. "I don't think there are enough hours in the day for Patience to be good enough to make the team," Dylan said coolly. She matched Lynsey's smile. "But I agree that the pony has potential. Maybe you could teach Minuet to memorize the course and then glue Patience to the saddle?"

Uh-oh, this can't be good. Honey swapped an uneasy look with Malory.

Lynsey shrugged. "Really, Dylan, I've thought you were a number of things, but I never had you down as the jealous type."

"Jealous!" Dylan's eyebrows shot up. "Of what?"

"Patience," Lynsey snapped. "She's got a famous dad and a fantastic pony, so now you've got to do everything you can to put her down to make sure she isn't more popular than you."

Honey laid her hand on Dylan's arm, hoping to calm her.

"This isn't about popularity," Dylan seethed, shaking off Honey's hand. "It's about one person trying to sabotage another. What she did was just plain wrong! At least if you had turned me in, you would have taken the credit for it."

Lynsey seemed to consider the backhanded compliment and then rolled her eyes. "Get over it. That midnight dare is so yesterday's news. You're starting to sound boring, Dylan, and if you keep it up, no one's going to want to hang out with you."

Before Dylan could reply, Lynsey turned on her heel and marched off.

Yikes, Honey thought. *I know Dylan and Lynsey will never be best friends, but do they have to work so hard at being worst enemies?*

Chapter Five

After dinner Honey emailed Sam. At least she had plenty of news for him, knowing how much he liked to hear about her life at school. Back in England they had shared many of the same friends. Still, Honey had been kind of surprised when Sam started asking questions about Dylan, Malory, and Lani, as if he had met them all.

Hey Sam,

Ok, first things first. I PROMISE I'll have a good rest of the term. Seriously, sometimes you act like you're six years older than me, not six minutes :-)

Things started right where they left off before the holi-day. Dylan and Patience are clashing already, and Lynsey seems to think Dylan should just get over it. I thought we were going to have to hold them back, but I don't think Lynsey wanted to risk her manicure.

Caleb emailed Malory and set up The Date, which goes by the code word coffee. We're all going to meet on Saturday. Malory acts like it's no big deal, but we all know different!

You'll never guess which horse I got to ride today. The senior captain's Thoroughbred, Mischief Maker! He's nothing like his name – or if he is, then he went really easy on me. He's so big Rocky would have been able to walk under his stomach, but I didn't feel nervous on him. Lani thinks I'm going to find it hard coming back down to riding the usual horses. I know you're not that into the horse stuff, but I have to tell you that Patience's dad bought her this gorgeous pony, Moonlight Minuet. Lynsey seems to think Patience will make the competition team now. Patience still has a hard time riding, but I bet Minuet could win a class without a rider.

So it's all go here, but you know I'm always thinking about you. We played a game of Monopoly last night, and I actually got to use the Boot because my friends aren't as selfish and controlling as my twin brother. But the Boot didn't bring me any luck – I lost all my money in about fifteen minutes flat – so you can definitely play with it next time.

I have to head off for a Christmas party planning session – very important for school spirit, you know.

Speak to you soon! (You can call or text me anytime. But I can't pick up in class – too bad.)

Lots of love,

Honeyxxx

Honey felt like it was a newsy, cheerful email, the kind any sister would send to her brother from school. But Honey and Sam weren't just any sister and brother, were they? They were twins, and one of them was sick

– really sick. Honey pressed send before she could change her mind and put what she really wanted to say in the email, like *How are you? Are you scared? Does it hurt a lot?* Everyone always said that twins were supposed to know what the other one was feeling, but Honey had no idea what Sam was going through, not even when the pain made him sick, or when he didn't sleep for days following his treatment. She hated knowing he was suffering and that he was struggling to make it seem like things were OK. They used to do just about *everything* together, which had seemed like the whole point of being twins, but he was dealing with this entirely without her.

She walked out of the student centre, realizing that the last thing they had done that had made them seem like twins, the last thing that made their parents roll their eyes and think there was some freakish genetic connection between them, was before Sam got sick. Nearly two years ago, Honey had broken her wrist, falling off Rocky. Sam had broken his wrist the exact same day in a rugby game. Honey had got back into the saddle as soon as the cast was taken off six weeks later. But Sam hadn't played rugby since. Not because of his wrist – it had healed as quickly as Honey's. But he had started to feel tired all the time, and then caught a cold that just never got better.

Honey felt her stomach turn over. It was so unfair. That had been when they'd discovered Sam was really sick. Honey had heard of leukemia before. She knew it was a kind of cancer, but she thought only old people got sick with it. Not her twin brother, who was only ten. They had broken their wrists together. Why hadn't they fallen sick together, too? She couldn't shake the guilty feeling that she had been the lucky one and didn't deserve to be.

Honey walked into the yard and across to the barn, which was brightly lit by large outdoor lanterns. Inside the electric lights were on, casting the stalls in a cosy yellow glow. As Honey wandered down the barn's centre aisle, she listened to the rhythmic munching of the horses digging into their evening hay nets and felt herself relax.

She stopped outside Minuet's stall. The mare was quietly pulling at her net, resting her hind leg underneath her. "Hey, Minnie," Honey said softly, holding out the horse buscuit she'd brought.

The grey pony swung her head around and pricked her ears. A moment later she left her net and rustled through her deep straw bed before stretching out her nose to lip the buscuit off Honey's palm. Once she'd finished crunching, Minuet stayed where she was, half closing her eyes while Honey scratched her forehead.

"You were pretty amazing today," Honey told her. "Most horses would have let Patience fall off, but you didn't want her to get hurt, did you?" Minuet's ears flickered at the sound of Honey's voice. She nodded her head when Honey moved her hand to rub around the base of her ear. "Do you like that?" Honey murmured, thinking Minnie was one of the most people-friendly horses she'd ever met. A lot of horses got fidgety if their ears were touched.

"OK girl, I'm going to go say hi to Kingfisher now," Honey told the mare.

Minuet rubbed her lip against Honey's sleeve and then gave it a tiny nibble. "Do you want me to stay a bit longer?" Honey laughed. *Maybe she's feeling a bit lonely. She might be missing her old home.*

"I'll comb your mane for you, but you'll have to let go of me first," Honey offered, gently pulling her sleeve away.

She fetched a comb and slipped into Minuet's stable to begin untangling her long, silver mane. "Your mane is just like one of the model horses I had when I was seven," Honey found herself confessing. "My brother collected rugby shirts, and I collected toy horses. You should have seen my bedroom at home. It was like a miniature stable yard! My dad even spent one summer painting a barn mural with a paddock and a fence on the wall. He always did stuff for us during his holidays. Once he bought us this massive paddling pool and inflated it right outside the back door. Of course, Sam accidentally punctured it with a plastic sword or lightsaber or something and the water flooded the kitchen!"

Minuet turned and nuzzled Honey's shoulder playfully. "I know, I know. You're wondering what I'm going on about," Honey said with a self-conscious laugh. She looked up as Sarah, one of the stable hands, peered over the door.

"Hey, Honey. I thought I heard someone in here. I

was about to turn the lights off."

"It's OK. I should get going," Honey said, wondering if she should explain what she was doing there. "I wanted to make sure Minuet was settling in OK. Everything seems fine."

"OK, then, if you're ready, I'll get the lights."

Honey stepped out of the stall as Sarah headed to the main switch in the tack room. "I have to go," she told Minuet. "I'll come and see you again soon, I promise." She hurried toward the doors, but every time she looked back, the mare was still watching her over the stable door. *You sure are a people pony*, Honey thought, smiling.

She fished out her mobile as she headed back to the dorm. She wanted to give her parents a quick call before her meeting. She'd deliberately kept herself from bombarding Sam with questions in her email, but she was desperate to check with her parents about how he was doing.

"'Lo," someone answered on the other end.

Sam!

"What way to answer the phone is that?" Honey teased. "I swear I got all the manners in the family."

"And I got all the good looks."

"You know, there isn't a law that says you have to like your twin."

"Oh, yeah?" Sam sounded amused.

He sounded so normal it was hard to remember how sick he was. Honey pressed the receiver closer to her ear, wishing she could somehow be closer to him.

"What's up?" Sam asked when she didn't respond.

"I emailed you with all the news," Honey told him. "Didn't you read it yet?"

"I don't live online! So you emailed me, and now you're calling. Missing me that much, huh?"

"That ego of yours is out of control." Honey laughed. "I thought you'd be in bed. I was calling to talk to Mum and Dad."

"What you mean is you thought I'd be in bed and you were calling up to check up on me," Sam replied.

"You got me there," Honey admitted.

"I'm OK, so stop stressing," Sam said. "You've got enough to worry about trying to keep your marks up with mine."

Sam was being home-tutored by their mother; Honey thought how much different it could have been if he had been at Saint Kits. She would have seen him at the show-jumping event last week, and they could have met up in town on Saturdays. But that was what regular brothers and sisters did. She probably would never get to do it with Sam.

"Very funny," she said sarcastically. "Now stop trying to avoid the question and tell me how you really are."

"Oh you know, I'm kind of tired. We can't all live an easy life at boarding school, with dozens of servants to fetch and carry for us. So I was just about to go to bed."

Honey's fingers tightened around her mobile phone as she pictured her brother in his pyjamas. It wasn't even eight o'clock yet. "Put me on to Mum, then. You need your beauty sleep."

"Well if you hadn't kept me on the phone, I'd be in bed by now." Sam couldn't resist one final tease.

"Go!" Honey exclaimed.

She took a deep breath as Sam said good-bye and called their mother to the phone. *How does he stay so upbeat? she wondered. I wish he would be honest with me instead of trying to put on an act that everything's OK. Why can't he tell me if he's scared, if he's hurting, if he ever wonders why he was the one who is sick? We used to tell each other everything.*

"Hi, Honey." Her mom came on the phone. "Are you OKk?"

"Yeah, just wanted to check in with Sam and you and Dad," Honey replied.

"We're fine," her mom said reassuringly. "I wasn't expecting you to call this evening. Remember what we promised?"

"I won't worry, and you'll phone me if there's any news," Honey recited. She wanted to tell her mother exactly how she felt, but the last thing she wanted was to add to her parents' worries. She'd never forget the first time she heard her mom cry. It had been after Sam's first bout of chemotherapy. Honey had listened to her mom sob through the bedroom wall late at night, while her dad helplessly tried to comfort her. She had sworn from that moment on she would do everything she could not to make her parents worry about her, although she hadn't realized she'd be promising herself the same thing a second time around.

She heard herself saying brightly, "I'm having a great

time. I got to ride Mischief Maker, the senior team captain's horse, today!"

"Hey, that sounds exciting! Tell me all about it."

"He was amazing, Mum, like driving a Rolls-Royce when all you've ever practised in is a Ford!" She tailed off as her mom cupped her hand over the receiver to shout to her dad.

"I've already got his medication out. It's on the kitchen counter." Mrs Harper gave her attention back to Honey. "I'm glad you've settled straight back in."

"Absolutely. I don't have any time to get homesick," Honey agreed, knowing how important it was that her mom thought she was happy at Chestnut Hill. *I am happy here, but I just wish I could be with my family right now. I wish there was something I could do.* "Anyway, I'd better go. We've got a meeting about the dorm Christmas party."

"A Christmas party? That sounds fun! I'll want to hear all about the plans," said her mom.

No you won't, Honey thought mutinously, then told herself to stop being a brat. She knew her mom would ask all the right questions, but how could she care about riding lessons and Christmas parties when Sam. . . Honey bit her lip as the thought of Sam at a hospital Christmas party flashed through her mind.

"We'll call you the moment there's any news," her mother promised again. "Have fun planning your big party."

After Honey hung up, she pulled open the foyer door and stopped in the hallway, taking deep breaths to calm herself. The reason her parents had sent her to Chestnut Hill was because they hated the thought of Honey being alone for hours while they took Sam to hospital appointments and looked after him. Honey had argued at first that she wanted to be there for Sam, but her parents had been adamant that she needed to be away at school where she could enjoy making friends and do all the things they didn't have time to do with her. Honey had finally agreed, because she could see how important it was to her parents to feel that they were doing their best by her. She remembered visiting the campus and how impressed her mom had been with the landscaped grounds and colonial buildings. Honey leaned against the wooden archway that led to the senior sitting room and took another deep breath to get her bearings.

"Honey, over here!" Lani waved to her from the study corner, where dark oak desks had been pushed back against the bookshelves to make space.

"Um, are you going in?" Susanna and Carrie James, twins in their freshman year, spoke behind Honey.

"Sorry!" Honey apologized, stepping into the room. "I was just admiring the view." The senior sitting room was at least double the size of the seventh- and eighth-graders' lounge. It was L-shaped, with game tables in one section, and a full kitchen!

"It's pretty neat," Susanna agreed. "We've been trying to get them to set up a freshman time-share, but so far they haven't bitten. I guess you feel like you've earned it once you're a senior."

Honey followed the twins past a cluster of sofas and chairs around a giant plasma TV screen and took a seat between Alexandra and Lani.

"Here." Alex handed her a notepad and pen. "I thought I'd get you one before they all disappeared."

"Thanks." Honey took the pad, noticing that just about everyone else had one, too.

The seniors had managed to make enough room for them all to sit in a large square. It was the first time that the Adams girls had gathered together as the entire dorm, and Honey was surprised at how many people she recognized even though she had classes only with first- and second-years.

"We've decided against planning the Christmas party," Lani stage-whispered to Honey.

"Really?" Honey said in surprise.

"Absolutely." Dylan nodded. "We want to decide on strategy for taking over the senior sitting room instead."

"You'll have to wait your turn, just like we had to," said Noel Cousins, the senior prefect, overhearing them. "Although our hourly rental rates are reasonable."

"Yep, it should only cost about an average month's allowance," one of the senior team riders agreed, tucking her feet up on the sofa.

"Each," Noel added, her green eyes twinkling. She helped herself to a soda from a coffee table laden with snacks.

Another senior, Holly Leigh-Barber, stood up. "I think we're all here, so let's start," she announced, sounding very official.

Honey raised her eyebrows at Lani as Holly shushed a group of freshmen who were still chatting.

The senior started to run the meeting in a very formal manner, with individuals proposing possible themes for the Adams House holiday gathering. Girls pitched everything from a Hollywood look-alike gala to an old-fashioned sleigh-ride-style event. But in the end, everyone agreed that a classic fireside pyjama party – complete with stockings hung by the chimney with care, as well as biscuits and milk – would be cosy and fun. Plus, the senior sitting room had a real fireplace that would add ambience.

Honey noticed that while most girls looked very pleased with the arrangements, Holly Leigh-Barber was still standing in front of the room, trying to get the group to focus.

"That's all fine, you guys, but we still haven't come up with any ideas for our Christmas party beyond pyjamas," Holly reminded them. "Don't you think we need a little more?"

"How about we have some kind of game?" Lucy suggested.

"My mom held a surprise party for my dad's fortieth this summer," Noel said. "She got all the guests to bring baby pictures. She pinned them up on a board, and people had to match the right baby with the right adult."

"That would be so cool," Razina enthused. "We could get our parents to send us photos if we don't have them."

"I don't mind organizing the game if you all bring in your photos. Just make sure you put your names on the back if you want them returned," Noel added. "Let's do one baby and one current, so people can try to –compare."

"Great. Now all we have to arrange is who's going to do the food, decorations, and music," Holly said, scribbling on her pad.

"Oh, minor details." Dylan grinned. But Honey knew Dylan would be first to volunteer for the food committee.

When the warning bell rang for underclassmen lights-out, the students had all the party details wrapped up and were returning to their rooms.

"How about we get out some photos tonight?" Dylan suggested to Honey as they reached their room. "I'm dying to see how easy it is to match your baby picture with you as you are now. I'm guessing pretty easy. Your face is so distinctive."

"What's your hurry?" Honey said evasively. "We can look at them tomorrow." The truth was Honey didn't want to get her album out with the others around. Just about every page had photos of Sam on it.

Lani stopped with them in front of their room. "Hey, guys, anyone else going to have a hard time sleeping? I just napped through that whole meeting. Did it have to be so long?"

"Come on," Dylan said enthusiastically. "At least we ended up with good ideas. I'm just trying to persuade

Honey to pick out a baby photo right now."

"Excellent plan," Lani said as she opened the door and led the way into the room, followed by Malory.

"The second bell's about to ring!" Honey protested.

"We've still got another ten minutes." Malory sat down on Honey's bed and scooped up her plush bear, Woozle. "I'd like to see it."

"Yeah, cough it up, Honey," Lani said. "Or we'll have to sacrifice the bear."

"C'mon, Hon, don't be a spoilsport," Dylan added. She gestured to the photos of Rocky on Honey's section of the pin board. "We already know you have the best picture collection of all of us."

"Maybe Honey's not photogenic," Lani teased. "This could be her greatest fear."

Honey pretended to swat her, but she could tell that she wasn't going to get out of this one. She quickly pulled her album out of her bedside drawer. Maybe if she was quick enough, she could grab a photo before the others tried to flip through the rest of the pictures. She sat cross-legged on her bed and lifted the album onto her lap. As she tilted the heavy album, a loose photo slid out and fell facedown on the carpet.

Dylan bent down and picked it up. "Hey, this would be a good one for the competition!"

"You look so cute!" Malory exclaimed, plucking the photo from Dylan's hand. "You're Woozle size!"

Honey leaned over to look at the photo. Lying on a blanket alongside her teddy bear, Woozle, was a blond-haired baby, kicking its legs and smiling up at the camera. The only problem was that the baby wasn't Honey. It was Sam.

"Why are you wearing a blue romper?" Lani asked in a confused voice. "Were your parents expecting you to be a boy?"

Honey knew she couldn't keep Sam a secret any longer. Her pulse raced as she tried to imagine her friends' reactions when they heard she had a brother she hadn't mentioned for almost an entire term. And not just any brother – a twin!

Her mouth felt dry as she tried to find the right words. "Actually, that's not me. It's Sam, my twin brother."

Chapter Six

"You have a twin? Oh my gosh, that is so cool!" Dylan exclaimed, her eyes opening wide.

"How come you've never told us about him before?" Malory stared at Honey in astonishment.

"You never asked," Honey told her lightly, hoping her friends wouldn't start interrogating her.

Dylan frowned. "Don't the two of you get along?"

"Of course we do," Honey said, taking the photo and pushing it back into the album.

Dylan held up her hands. "You don't need to get testy. You have to admit it's pretty weird that you haven't mentioned him before. If I had a twin, there's no way I'd keep it secret."

"Well, you'd have a hard time keeping anything secret," Malory told her. "There's no rule that says we have to declare relatives."

"Yeah, look at me. I do everything I can to deny all knowledge of my sisters," Lani said, grinning. "Anytime you feel like adopting some siblings, I have three that you could have!"

"Do you have any photos of your brother now?" Dylan persisted.

Honey knew she couldn't deflect their curiosity forever, and she didn't want them to think she hadn't talked about Sam before because she didn't like him. "Sure."

She looked through the album, being careful not to flip too far, and found one of Sam just before he got sick. He was wearing a mud-streaked rugby uniform and holding a silver trophy high in the air, his blond hair clinging damply to his forehead. A group of boys clustered around him, all with jubilant expressions on their faces. "This is his team winning the South London Junior Rugby Tournament the summer before last. He's in the centre."

The girls crowded closer to take a look. "Um, yeah," Malory agreed. "You guys look alike."

"He's cute." Lani let out a low whistle. "No wonder you wanted to keep him secret – you knew we'd all start plaguing you to set up a date."

Honey held up her hands in mock surrender. She was happy to let her friends think she was trying to hide her brother because he was such a catch. "You got me!"

"Well, the truth's out now, and you can put me at the top of the list for a coffee with him," Dylan teased.

"So, are the two of you, like, telepathic?" Malory asked, sitting on Honey's bed and hugging her knees.

Honey smiled and shook her head. "Most of the time he's just like a regular brother. You know, we fight and get on each other's nerves. But sometimes we come out with the same thought, or pick up the phone at the same second. When we were younger we always used to pretend to be psychic. It was amazing how many people fell for it."

"Do you like the same food?" Dylan asked.

"Does he ride, too?" Lani demanded.

"What is this? Fifty questions?" Honey laughed uneasily.

"You can't just drop the fact that you have a twin on us and then expect to get away without a full-on interrogation," Dylan warned. "Especially not when he's so ... well ... *hot!*"

"Well, I hate to tell you, but Sam doesn't like nosy, prying girls." Honey tried to keep a bantering tone as she shoved the album back into her cabinet. "So since Malory has asked the fewest questions, I'll have to put her at the top of the list for this date." *Please fall for the change of subject*, Honey thought as she mentally crossed her fingers.

"But Mal's already spoken for! It's only three days until her big date with Caleb," Dylan reminded them.

"Thanks for bringing that up. I still haven't decided what to wear," Malory sighed.

"Maybe we should pool our clothes. It's not like you're going to have a chance to go shopping before Saturday," Dylan pointed out.

The second bell rang, and Lani looked at Mal. "We'd better get going before Hersie comes around."

"Yeah, pj's at warp speed," Malory agreed.

The door opened, and the girls held their breath as if they expected Mrs Herson, their housemother, to appear just because her name had been spoken.

"You'd better get going, the second bell's rung," Lynsey said unnecessarily as she entered the room. She headed straight for her vanity unit, pulling her hair free from its braid and running her fingers through it before picking up her monogrammed hairbrush. She always spent at least ten minutes brushing her hair before putting it up for bed.

"Don't worry, we're out of here," Lani said. "See you in the morning, guys." She followed Malory out the door but ducked her head back in and shot Honey a grin. "I think you're lucky to have Sam! I'd swap my sisters for one brother any day. Especially one that plays rugby!"

No deal! Honey wanted to shout.

Dylan waited until Lynsey headed to the bathroom, carrying her blue silk sleep chemise, and then sat on Honey's bed. "I'm sorry if I sounded kind of pushy back there."

"That's OK," Honey said, picking up Woozle and hugging his floppy body to her chest. "Forget it. I'm glad you all know."

"Maybe I was just jealous because I don't have any brothers or sisters," Dylan admitted, reaching over to brush the fur away from the teddy's stitched-on eyes. "I've always thought being a twin must be amazing – you know, the whole psychic, joined-at-the-hip thing. Maybe it doesn't work that way when one of you is a boy and the other a girl. I guess it must be like having a regular brother – and we all know how annoying boys can be. I get so frustrated with Nat I could scream, and he's only my cousin!"

Honey couldn't decide if it was better to let Dylan think that she and Sam weren't that close, or correct her and reignite the game of fifty questions.

Before she could make up her mind, Lynsey reappeared in her chemise, wiping a cotton ball over her cheeks. "You know, you two are cruising straight toward a detention if you're still dressed when Mrs Herson comes in."

Dylan and Honey scrambled off the bed. "Twenty seconds, and I'll be done," Honey promised, rummaging under her pillow for her striped pyjamas.

"Bet I can do it in ten," Dylan challenged, kicking off her Pumas. "Oops!" One of her trainers landed on Lynsey's bed.

"Give us all a break and calm down, Dylan," Lynsey sighed. "Not everything has to be an exhibition."

Dylan was about to reply when the door handle turned. "Beds!" she squeaked.

In one lightning-quick move, Honey was under her duvet, pulling the sheets up to her chin to hide the fact she was still fully dressed.

"How did your Christmas party planning go?" Mrs Herson popped her head around the door just as Honey noticed Dylan's duvet wasn't covering her legs – her jeans and orange socks were in full view.

"Really great, thanks," Lynsey replied, sitting smugly

up in bed with her hair tucked into a stretchy velvet band.

"I'll look forward to hearing more about it tomorrow," their housemother said before snapping off the light. "Oh, and Dylan. . ."

"Yes, Mrs Herson?" Dylan's sheets were also pulled up tight, her chestnut hair fanned over the top.

"You appear to have forgotten that it's customary to get undressed before going to bed. Maybe you could reconsider the role of pyjamas by tomorrow night? If not, then a detention might help you remember proper bedtime attire."

Honey snorted with laughter, quickly biting into her quilt to muffle the sound.

"Yes, Mrs Herson." Dylan sounded subdued, but the moment their housemother shut the door, she sat up in bed and lobbed a pillow at Honey. "How come you didn't get caught?"

"I'm obviously better at deception than you! It must be one of my hidden talents," Honey replied, lobbing the pillow back before they both collapsed with laughter. It took her a second to realize how true her statement was. She was still keeping a lot from her friends.

"That's enough, guys," Lynsey complained, clicking off her bedside lamp. "Some of us need our sleep. I've got to be fresh for the All Schools League and hockey training."

"We did warn you not to try out for two teams," Dylan reminded her, wriggling out of bed and scooping up her pyjamas.

Honey felt a jab of concern about the dark circles under Lynsey's eyes, clearly visible now that she didn't have any concealer on. "We'll be one minute, I promise," she said, jumping out of bed and grabbing Dylan's elbow. She marched her friend into the bathroom. "You have the All Schools League to practise for, too, you know."

"All Schools League, Christmas party, Mal's date," Dylan said, counting on her fingers. "We've got a lot to look forward to!"

"Hang on. It's only our first term" Honey laughed as she picked up her toner and dabbed it onto a cotton ball before smoothing it over her face. But she had to agree. The pace of life at Chestnut Hill was picking up more and more. Sometimes all you could concentrate on was trying to keep up.

When Honey woke the next morning, something felt different. What had changed? Then she remembered: *Sam's not a secret now*. She felt torn between relief that she didn't have to hide her twin any longer and concern that her friends were going to dig around and discover how sick he was. The reasons she hadn't mentioned him before remained: she didn't want people to feel sorry for her or treat her differently because her brother was sick, and she didn't want to have to talk about it with everyone.

She was almost relieved when their teachers loaded them down with work that day. It meant that her friends didn't have the chance to pick up on their questioning from the night before. *I never thought I'd be glad to get extra algebra problems*, she thought as she spread her books across the corner table in the student centre. They had made the drastic decision to work through their morning break, since they also had a major chemistry assignment due at the end of the week.

"Don't they realize we just got back from a holiday?" Dylan moaned. "They should be easing us in gently."

"It's shock tactics to get the holiday spirit whipped out of us," Lani agreed.

"Quit talking, you guys. I'd just figured out how a equals e over d, and now I have to start over," Malory complained, putting a line through her work.

"Well, when you figure it out again, can you tell me how you did it?" Honey begged.

Sam had always been amazing at maths. When they'd been at school together in Wimbledon, they'd had a pact where he'd do Honey's maths while she did his English. Even when they hadn't been allowed to sit next to each other, Sam kept coming up with ingenious ways to keep helping Honey. She bit back a smile as she remembered the time he'd scribbled answers on his palm and then gone up to their teacher's desk to ask a question. He held his hands behind his back for her to see, but she couldn't see what he'd written because he was so far away – plus he had atrocious handwriting. Their dad said it looked like spiders with muddy feet doing a waltz, which sounded so absurd it just made Honey and Sam laugh.

By the time Honey finished her study period at the end of the day, her head felt so crammed full of a mixture of algebra and the Civil War that she couldn't wait to get out into the fresh air. Dylan, Lani, and Malory had decided to pitch some balls down on the softball field. Honey had been tempted to go with them, but ball sports had never been her thing; plus she couldn't resist popping in to see Minuet. *I've missed her today,* she thought, crunching over the half-frozen lawn. The temperature was stubbornly staying below freezing, even though it was barely December. Honey had all her fingers crossed for a white Christmas. *Sam would love that.*

When Honey approached the outdoor arena, she could see the floodlights were on. She guessed it was one of the members of staff, working their own horse after school hours. When she got closer, Honey felt a stab of surprise to see Lynsey standing in the middle of the arena with Patience cantering a figure of eight on Minuet. *Minnie has the most amazing outline,* Honey thought, watching the snow-coloured pony flex her neck to accept the bit. *But how come they're riding without an instructor?*

"We've got permission to be here, so don't stress," Lynsey called as if she had read Honey's mind. "Try her over the jump now," she went on, turning back to Patience.

Honey frowned. The combination fence set up at the far end of the arena looked way too high. Patience would do better with low, easy fences to get her confidence up. Honey thought fast. "Do you want me to lower it into two cross poles so Minnie can warm up?" she suggested diplomatically.

"No. One of the reasons Patience's dad bought her was because of her jumping ability. It's not like a fence of this size is going to be a problem for her," Lynsey shouted back.

"But it might be a problem for Patience," Honey murmured as she watched Minuet approach the combination in a steady canter. The mare tucked her legs up close as she sailed over the first jump. She needed to take three strides before the second fence, but Patience lurched forward as they landed. She pulled at Minuet's reins as she tried to regain her balance, and the mare's stride faltered. *She's not going to make it*, Honey realized as Minuet got much too close to the second fence. The mare knew it, too, and swerved to the side instead of attempting the jump. Patience fell awkwardly onto Minnie's neck and pushed herself back up, looking frustrated.

"Take her over again," Lynsey called.

Lower the fences! Honey begged silently. She knew Patience had a better chance of keeping her balance over the fences if they weren't so high.

Patience turned Minuet to face the jump again, but she was holding her too tight. The grey mare shook her head, trying to lengthen her stride, but Patience pulled her back even more. *Come on; she needs her head free to get over.*

It was no great surprise when Minuet skidded to a halt in front of the first fence.

"Bad girl!" Patience said, smacking Minuet's neck and ramming her heels against the pony's sides.

"Let me take her over," Lynsey said. "She's getting stressed."

Honey was glad that Lynsey had noticed the damp sheen on Minuet's coat. She watched as Patience slid off. Lynsey adjusted her stirrups and took Patience's riding helmet before mounting. Honey knew Lynsey was doing the right thing by taking the mare once over the fence so the session didn't end on a failure. The mare needed to boost her confidence.

Lynsey trotted Minuet in a circle before turning her at the jump. The mare flew over the first fence, and Lynsey followed her movement perfectly to set her up nicely for the second rail. Minnie sailed over, swishing her tail when she landed.

She's some jumper, Honey thought admiringly. She waited for Lynsey to slow the grey mare to a walk and cool her down. But instead Lynsey cantered in a circle and came at the jump again. Minnie flew over both fences just as perfectly.

"Good girl." Lynsey patted her neck. "Put the fences up," she called to Patience.

Honey frowned as Patience unhooked the cups on the fence standards and raised the poles. *Minnie's looking tired, like she needs a break.*

"See what I mean about her jumping ability?" Lynsey said smugly as she circled Minuet.

"She looks like she really enjoys it," Honey agreed. "That was a great jump to finish the session on," she added hopefully.

"Why quit when she's just hitting her stride? Let's see what she's made of." Lynsey kept circling Minuet until Patience stepped back from the jump. The mare formed a gorgeous arc over the higher fence, stretching out her neck as she easily cleared both rails.

Honey heard the gate click as Ms Phillips, the jumping coach, strode into the arena. "I'm sorry. That phone call took longer than I thought," she apologized, pushing her hand through her short blonde hair. "Is everything OK? Why aren't you on Minuet?" she asked Patience.

"I wanted to take her higher," Lynsey answered for Patience, reining the mare to a halt. "She's got a huge jump."

"Well, she looks as if she's done more than enough for one night," said Ms Phillips. "Cool her down and then put her away."

"Sure." Lynsey nodded.

While Lynsey walked Minuet around the arena on a loose rein, Honey went up to the barn to get a bucket and sponge ready for the mare.

"Oh, thanks." Patience sounded surprised when she led the mare into her stable and found Honey waiting for her.

"It's OK," Honey replied. "I thought it might save some time, since it's getting late." She helped Patience take off the saddle and bridle and hung them on the wall. "Is Lynsey coming to help?" she asked. She suspected Lynsey would be unimpressed to find Honey in Minuet's stall.

"She's outside talking to Ms Phillips about the cross-country course. She wants to know who the course builder's going to be. She needs to make sure the architect has good credentials. If Bluegrass injures himself on any jumps, he'll be off the show-jumping circuit this summer," Patience explained. She fished the sponge out of the bucket. "So, do I wash her all over?" She held the dripping sponge between her thumb and finger over Minuet's back. The mare shifted uneasily as some cold droplets fell onto her warm coat, but Honey noticed she was too well mannered to object more strongly.

"Not all over," she said quickly. "Just where her tack has been – where she's sweaty. But you need to squeeze out some of that water first. I've got another sponge for her eyes and nose."

She watched Patience hesitantly rub the sponge over Minnie's back. When the mare stamped her foot to shake loose some drips that were running down her leg, Patience jumped backward.

She really doesn't know how to look after her pony, Honey thought, taking the second sponge and gently wiping around Minuet's ears. The mare stood still while Honey sponged off all the sweat marks where the bridle had been. "Good girl," Honey praised her before going around to check on Patience.

"I think I might have overdone the water." Patience

made a face at the soaked patch on Minuet's back.

"It's OK." Honey reached into the grooming box for a pristine red plastic sweat scraper. "You can dry her off with this."

Patience hesitated a moment. "I've always wanted a white pony," she said as she angled the sweat scraper over Minnie's side. Honey looked up with a smile, wondering if she should explain that Minuet was technically a grey pony, since she had black skin and white hair – grey ponies could range from completely white to dark grey, including dapple. Honey decided not to say anything. It was a simple mistake that anyone who didn't really know horses might make.

After Patience had got rid of most of the water, Honey dried Minuet off with a stable rubber.

"I guess you're going to put her blanket back on now, right?" Patience asked. The question in her voice made it clear she wasn't about to do this herself.

She must know how to put Minnie's blanket on, Honey thought, pulling it off the wall. She threw it lightly over Minuet and buckled the chest straps, while Patience watched her like a hawk.

"Hurry up. The O.C.'s on in ten minutes," Lynsey called from the end of the aisle.

Patience looked at her tack and grooming kit and then at Honey.

"It's fine. I'll finish cleaning up here," Honey told her.

"Thanks." Patience smiled, letting herself out of the stall.

Honey scooped up Minuet's saddle and bridle and carried them to the tack room. The walls were lined with saddle racks with the ponies' names above them. Honey noticed that Patience had surrounded Minnie's name with small gold stars. *She obviously enjoys owning Minnie, but she doesn't understand anything about stable management*, Honey thought, hanging up the tack. For Honey the everyday routine of caring for a pony was the best part. It was when you really got to know the horse as a friend instead of as just a rider.

As she slotted the grooming kit into its space on the shelf, her mobile phone rang. Honey's heart started to race when she recognized her home number on the screen.

"Mum, is everything OK?"

"Yes, everything's fine!" Her mom sounded surprised by her question, and Honey bit back the familiar feeling of frustration. Why couldn't her parents understand how worried she was? "I tried to get hold of you earlier, but your phone was off. You were probably still in class. The hospital rang today with an appointment for Sam's first treatment of chemotherapy."

Honey's hand tightened around the phone. "When is it?"

"In two days," her mom told her. "A bit earlier than we'd expected, but it's good they can fit him in."

"How's Sam?"

"Oh, typical Sam. He's determined to keep positive over all of this. We all need to be brave for his sake, but you know that already, don't you, love?"

Honey nodded. Her brother was totally amazing; she didn't know if she'd be so brave if it was happening to her. "Can I speak to him?"

"He's gone to bed," her mom replied.

"Did he wear himself out today?"

"No, he wanted to watch a new DVD in his room." Honey heard a note of irritation in her mom's voice. "You shouldn't stress yourself, worrying over every little thing."

I wouldn't have to if you'd been open with me from the start about Sam's getting sick again. You knew the cancer had come back weeks before you decided to tell me.

Honey said good night and switched off her phone, wishing it had been her dad she'd spoken with. She'd always been close to her mother, but lately she'd been finding it hard to talk to her without there being some sort of fallout. Her mom was on a knife's edge worrying over Sam, and it didn't make for relaxing conversations. Her dad was just as worried, but his easy relationship with Honey hadn't changed. *Dad's always been so completely on our level,* Honey thought. Being a professor, Mr Harper's holidays had always coincided with Honey and Sam's; and he'd made sure they had some great times together. *Like that time he woke us up to go watch a badger family at midnight.* The twins had crouched in the crispy bracken on either side of their dad as four young badgers tumbled out of the darkness under the watchful eyes of their parents. The badgers had played in the moonlight with the babies, filling the still night air with cute growls as they pretended to fight. *Magic*.

Honey leaned against the wall, squeezing her eyes shut with pain. She and Sam might never share a moment like that again. *I just wish I could be at the hospital with him*. But the reason she was here was that there was absolutely nothing she could do to make her twin better. Zilch. Zero. Honey furiously blinked back her tears. She'd only be letting her parents down if she started to make a fuss about how she was feeling. She didn't want to be accused of making it harder on everyone else. There was no way she was going to let Sam be the strong one on his own.

She was walking up the aisle when Ms Phillips came in.

"Hello, Honey. I was just about to turn the lights off. Are Lynsey and Patience still here?"

"Um, I think they had something to do." Honey wasn't about to tell her they'd gone to watch TV and left her to finish up with Minuet.

Ms Phillips looked pointedly at Minnie's grey hair, clinging to Honey's trousers. "If they want to schedule in an extra riding session, then they're expected to see to their ponies afterward. It's not fair to expect Sarah or Kelly – or you – to take on the extra work."

"I don't mind. I enjoy spending time with Minuet," Honey said quickly.

"She's a sweet pony." Ms Phillips smiled before walking away.

She sure is, Honey thought, unable to resist popping

into the stall to give Minnie one final pat.

Minuet stopped eating from her hay net and turned to gaze straight at Honey. Then she did something Honey had never known a pony to do before. She actually curled her head and neck partway around Honey just like she was giving her a hug! Honey felt a thrill of delight as she slipped her arms around Minnie and returned the embrace. *She's more than just a pony. She's turning into a real friend.*

Chapter Seven

At Saturday morning breakfast, Honey chose a bowl of museli along with some plain yogurt. She hesitated over a cinnamon bagel but decided against it. She was too worried about Sam's chemo to eat much.

Alexandra and Lani made room for Honey to sit between them. Malory was finishing off a fruit salad and a scone. *At least her big date with Caleb's not affecting her appetite*, Honey thought.

Honey gazed down at her own breakfast. It might as well be a bowl of sawdust for all she felt like eating it. All she could think about was Sam's hospital appointment. *I should be there for him*.

"I think my Jimmy Choo boots will go really well with the wool dress you're going to wear," Dylan said, sitting down with a mug of fresh coffee. "I'll go get them for you to try on after breakfast."

"Thanks, Dyl," Malory said. "But actually I've decided against the dress. I think it's overkill for going to the mall."

"The good news is she's narrowed it down to a

shortlist of six outfits." Alexandra grinned.

"Our room looks like backstage at a fashion show," Lani added. "Anyone would think Paris Hilton spent the night."

"I've never had to think of outfits around Caleb before," Malory confessed. "He probably thinks my entire wardrobe is jodhs and sweatshirts."

"Come on," Honey said, shoving away her uneaten museli. "Show me the outfits that made it to the finals."

"You don't need to skip breakfast – the minibus doesn't leave for an hour," Dylan pointed out.

"It's OK, I'll grab some fruit on the way out," Honey promised. Right now she was looking forward to giving all her attention to Malory. It was one way of taking her mind off Sam.

"I just want to stop by the stable for a couple of minutes to check on Tybalt's legs," Malory said as they got ready to the leave the table. "It would have been pretty heavy going in the outdoor arena yesterday with all that rain." The temperature had finally risen above freezing, but there had been so much rain over the last two days that Dylan had complained of feeling like Mrs Noah, and started muttering about chopping up the lounge furniture to build a twenty-first-century ark.

"Sure, I'm more than happy to visit the barn." Honey smiled at the thought of being able to share her apple with Minuet.

"I'll do your hair as soon as I've finished up," Dylan promised.

"Me, too," Lani agreed. "Starbucks won't know what hit it."

Honey ran her hand over a brown wool jersey dress that was draped across Malory's bed. The fabric felt like pure cashmere, but Malory was right – it did look a little dressy for coffee at the mall. "Is this the one you decided against?"

Malory nodded. "But I don't want to go too far the other way and let Caleb think I've made zero effort." She picked up a hoodie. "I thought about this and jeans, but then I won't look any different from any other time I go to the mall."

"You could always go in your pj's," Honey said mischievously, looking at Malory's pyjamas folded on top of her pillow.

"At least I might score points for originality!" Malory laughed. "Maybe I should just go with the dress to save time. Dylan will be here to do my hair in a minute, and she won't let me move for like an hour."

"I can do your makeup at the same time," Honey reminded her. "I was thinking of going for the barely there look, as opposed to Cleopatra. Although you might have a problem stopping Lani from doing the hieroglyphics on your arms again." They had all pitched in to help Malory get into costume for the Halloween party; and she'd made a fantastic Egyptian queen, complete with a toga, chunky gold-coloured jewellry, and intense eyeliner.

Malory made a face. "You know, this is all starting to

feel a little too complicated. I mean, I hung out with Caleb all summer! Won't he think it's weird if I start dressing like someone else?"

"We won't make you look like someone else," Honey promised. "Just a particularly good version of yourself!" She pulled open Malory's closet doors. "How about teaming up a kind of fancy top with jeans?" she suggested. She pulled out Malory's favourite pair of jeans and an aqua-coloured shirt with sheer sleeves.

"Good idea," Malory said, nodding enthusiastically. "Denim has never done me wrong."

"Which idea would that be?" Dylan asked, walking in with Lani and Alexandra.

"Going for sassy *and* casual," Honey said, holding the jeans and top against Malory.

Dylan reached out and fingered the tunic top. "It's pretty cold out there. Do you think Caleb will go for the blue lips, red nose look?"

"That won't happen if you borrow my new coat," Lani said.

"Your red trench coat!" Malory exclaimed. "Are you sure?"

"Totally," Lani said, unhooking the beautifully tailored coat from the back of her closet door.

"Go try everything on!" Dylan said, flapping her hands at Malory. "We've got forty-five minutes to do your hair and makeup before the shuttle leaves."

"It's cool, you guys!" Malory laughed. "Caleb's used to seeing me with my hair all sweaty and matted by a hard hat. If you make me look like I've just walked out of a salon, he'll think it's the wrong girl."

When Malory came out of the bathroom wearing her faded hip-slung jeans and the floaty aqua tunic, the girls whistled.

"That's the one," Alex declared. "You look perfect."

Honey tossed a hairbrush up into the air and deftly caught it. "Now let's get going with the rest of your makeover," she urged. "Do it for our sakes. We've all been looking forward to this date for weeks!" She told herself how interested Sam would be to hear all about Malory's Big Date with Caleb. *Maybe Mum and Dad were right to send me away after all. At least this way I get lots of upbeat news to share with Sam. That has to do him some good, right?*

"Aren't you going in?" Dylan teased when Malory hesitated in the doorway to the coffee shop.

Honey stopped just before she bumped into Dylan.

"Sorry!" Lani gasped as she collided into the back of Honey. "What's the hold-up?"

"Mal's thinking of pulling a Houdini," Dylan explained over her shoulder.

"My hair feels funny," Malory fretted, reaching up to run her hand over her new straightened style. "Does it look OK?"

"Not if you keep doing that," Honey said, pulling Malory's hand away. "You look terrific, really."

"And he's not here yet," Dylan added, peering through the window. "So maybe we can quit freezing out here?"

Malory gave an exaggerated sigh. "OK, guys. I'm going in."

"About time. I'm sure mall security had us tagged as suspicious," Lani joked as they headed into the shop. "No one in her right mind would stand outside in this weather."

"No one ever said Malory is in her right mind," Dylan pointed out.

Malory nudged Dylan indignantly, and they went to claim a corner booth while Honey and Lani ordered cappuccinos. By the time Lani put the tray down on the table, Dylan and Malory had taken off their coats and folded them over the back of the leather booth sofa.

The shop's front door opened, and all the girls looked over in the same instant. Two women walked in, weighed down with bags of items from Christmas shopping.

Malory caught Honey's eye and grinned self-consciously. "Maybe Caleb's caught sight of the new me and made a great escape."

"Um, I don't think so. Not from where I'm sitting anyway," said Lani, who had the best view out of the window from her corner seat.

The door opened again, and Honey squeezed Malory's arm as Caleb looked around the coffee shop. There were two other boys with him, one blond and one with dark brown hair.

Dylan waved. "Over here!"

"Cute friends," Lani muttered out of the corner of her mouth.

Honey had met one of the boys in town before, on a trip to the movies. His name was Josh, she remembered, looking at his pale blond hair and bright green eyes. She didn't recognize the taller, dark-haired boy.

"Hi," Caleb said as he stopped by their table.

His eyes met Malory's, and Honey was amused at the way his high cheekbones flushed red. *I wonder if he considered as many outfit combinations as Mal, getting ready for today?* Whether he had or not, Caleb looked relaxed but cute in his dark blue jeans and close-fitting white T-shirt.

"Um, meet Josh and Dan, my chaperones." Caleb introduced his friends.

"Lani, Honey, and Dylan," Malory said quickly, looking a bit self-conscious.

Honey and Dylan shifted closer to the window to make room for Josh and Dan to sit on their side of the table.

"I'll get some drinks. Anyone for a refill?" Josh offered before he sat down.

"We're all set, thanks." Dylan smiled, picking up her drink and sipping it.

"So," Caleb said, taking the seat next to Malory. "Did you have a good Thanksgiving?"

"As good as any vacation can be without riding," she replied with a grin.

"No kidding! I couldn't wait to get back to the barn to see Gent." Caleb's eyes lit up at the mention of Pageant's Pride, the long-legged grey gelding he rode for the Saint Kits junior team.

"He's gorgeous. He reminds me of Knight from Cheney Falls. Do you remember him?" Malory asked.

Caleb nodded. "He was the sixteen-two Thoroughbred, right? The one Elaine used for advanced dressage?"

"Yeah," Malory went on. "He did the most amazing demonstration for the Open House in August after you left."

Caleb shrugged. "Gent isn't much for dressage; but put any jump in front of him, and he's in horse heaven!"

I keep forgetting they hung out at Malory's stable this summer. I should have known they'd have tons to talk about! Honey swapped a grin with Lani at how quickly Malory and Caleb had become oblivious to the rest of them.

"That's ten bucks you owe me," Dan announced as Josh arrived back at the table with a tray of coffees.

"C'mon, Dan, not already," Josh groaned, sitting down next to Honey.

"Yep, a grand total of one minute and sixteen seconds," Dan declared, taking his coffee.

Lani raised her eyebrows. "Are you two going to let us in on the details of the bet?"

"Dan wagered that it would take them under three minutes before they started with the horse talk. I thought it would be more like four," Josh explained and then rolled his eyes in Caleb's direction. "He has no restraint."

"What's up?" Caleb broke off from his conversation

with Malory as they all burst out laughing.

"Horse talk. These guys were taking bets on how long it would take you two to get to your mutually favourite topic!" Lani teased.

"You mean there are other things to talk about?" Caleb asked in mock surprise. "OK. . . Hey, Malory, would you like to hear about the chemistry test I flunked this week? Or maybe we can discuss how ordinary people have the power to combat global warming?"

Malory laughed and propped her chin on her hand, pretending to look fascinated. Honey relaxed. Malory was clearly having a great time.

"We've met before somewhere, right?" Josh said to Honey, his green eyes friendly. "Outside the cinema a few weeks ago?"

Honey nodded.

"I think you guys ended up ditching the cineplex and going bowling instead," Josh went on. "Do you like bowling?"

Honey was about to reply when her mobile phone vibrated in her pocket. "Sam," she said under her breath. She stood up quickly and started to push her way past everyone in the booth. "I'm sorry," she said to Josh. "I have to take this."

Honey pushed her way out from the table and headed outside. "How did the chemotherapy go?" she demanded.

"It was OK. I knew you'd be worrying, so I thought I'd call you straightaway." Sam sounded exhausted. With a flash of guilt, Honey realized she'd hardly thought about what he'd been going through all morning. She'd let herself get distracted by helping Malory get ready for her date, and then talking with Josh.

"Mum and Dad are just driving me home now," Sam explained, his words slurring together.

"I wish I could be there," Honey said softly. She knew the side effects of chemotherapy could be pretty tough. It wasn't just losing his hair. When he'd had chemo before, Sam's appetite had vanished, and he'd lost tons of weight, when, with their slight frames, neither he nor Honey had much to spare in the first place. He'd had a pretty bad fever, too, and at one point his temperature had spiked to forty one degrees. Honey had spent hours with him, putting damp cloths on his head, nursing him with sips of cold drinks, and reading to him when he couldn't sleep.

"I'm glad you're not going to be here. As soon as I get home, I'm going to hit the sack, and you know you can never stop talking." Sam rallied enough to tease her.

Honey made herself smile, knowing he needed her to be as brave and cheerful as he was being. "Well, just to prove you wrong, I'm only going to talk for about twenty minutes this time. You'll never guess where I am! In town, outside the coffee shop. It's Malory's first date with Caleb, remember?"

"Yeah, I remember," Sam said dully.

Honey got the impression he was too tired to share her excitement. She bit her lip. Why should she even expect Sam to be interested? He'd never met Mal, or

Caleb, or any of her friends. Maybe she'd got it wrong, and he was sick of her going on and on about Chestnut Hill when he had bigger things to think about.

"Get some rest. I'll talk to you later," she told him before clicking off.

She leaned against the shop's window and sighed, her breath a frosty exhale. Suddenly the last place she wanted to be was inside, laughing and joking with her friends. It felt wrong that she could be out having fun while Sam was going through so much pain. She closed her eyes and let the cold seep into her.

We're twins; we're supposed to share everything. If I could switch places with him right now, I would. Why couldn't it have been me? Why did it have to be Sam?

"You've been quiet ever since you got that phone call." Dylan leaned across the minibus aisle to speak to Honey. "Was it from home? Is there a problem?"

"No, everything's fine." Honey made herself smile. "It was just my brother."

"I think Josh was about to ask you out bowling. But then he dropped it. I bet he thought the call was from your boyfriend," Dylan told her.

"But that's OK, because he hit on me instead, and we're going out on a date next Saturday," Lani added.

"No way!" Honey exclaimed at exactly the same time as Malory, who had been looking dreamily out of the window till now.

"You're kidding me, right?" Dylan said, her eyes opening wide.

94

"Right." Lani grinned. "But it was worth it to see the expressions on your faces. Besides, it's been the only thing that has pulled Malory out of her trance since we left."

"So are you seeing him again?" Honey asked.

Malory blushed and nodded. "He said we could set something up when we see each other at the All Schools competition next week."

"Way to go!" Dylan gave her a high-five.

"He is totally cute," Lani said, "plus he knows his way around a horse. A real catch, if you ask me."

Malory laughed. "You sound like my grandma! I don't think we use terms like that anymore."

"Yeah, Lani," Dylan scolded. "Women no longer catch men. It's all about equal partnership and mutual understanding."

Honey smiled at Dylan's obvious display of political correctness and leaned back against her seat. She was really happy for Mal, and it had been nice hanging out with Josh and Dan, too. Dan was an intermediate rider and had told a funny story about his first time trying countercanter. She thought she had overheard that Josh played lacrosse, but she had spaced out on the rest of that conversation. She sighed. She knew how important it was to her family that she continue with normal stuff, like hanging out with her friends at the mall. But there was no magic pill she could take to stop worrying about her twin – or for feeling guilty about getting on with her life when Sam couldn't.

When the minivan dropped the girls back at school, rain was pouring down. Part of her wanted to go back with the others to the dorm, where they'd drink hot chocolate, discuss Mal's date, and watch a DVD. But another part of her wanted to put some distance between herself and her friends. Something about the solitude of a walk in the rain appealed to her. Why should she go and enjoy herself when the effects of Sam's chemo would be kicking in at any moment? She might get cold and wet on her walk, but really, that was nothing.

Pulling her jacket closer, she decided to head down to the lake; but halfway down the path, a flash of white caught the corner of her eye. Honey peered toward the outdoor arena on the nearest side of the stable yard. Patience was trotting Minuet in a twenty-metre circle. The mare's nose was tucked to her chest; and even from a distance, Honey could tell the mare was having to work hard to lift her hooves out of the waterlogged sand.

She ran over to the fence. "Why don't you use the indoor ring?" she said breathlessly to Lynsey, who was watching Patience.

"Ms Phillips is schooling Scooby," Lynsey replied, pulling her hood closer over her hair.

"But the sand looks really wet. It's so deep. Patience should take her in," Honey said. She knew she was close to provoking Lynsey. She knew she shouldn't be interfering, but she was too concerned about Minuet to stop. How could she just stand by and do nothing?

"I know what I'm doing when it comes to training horses so they are in peak condition." Lynsey sounded irritated. "Minuet's got to be schooled every day if she's going to reach her full potential. Anyway, she's refusing to extend her trot for Patience. If we stop now, she'll think she can get away with giving less than one hundred per cent whenever Patience is riding her."

Honey looked at the mare, who had her ears back and her head lowered against the rain. *She's not enjoying this at all. This is no way for a horse to reach any kind of potential.*

Patience trotted over. "Honey, are you stalking my pony? Whenever we're down here with her, you appear. It's kind of spooky." Her smile was brittle. Clearly, she suspected Honey was checking up on her.

"I was just passing by." Honey winced at how lame her excuse sounded. *And on the subject of lame*, she thought, *Something's wrong with Minnie. She's standing awkwardly on her hindquarters, like her forelegs are aching. . .* "Minnie looks kind of stiff. Are you going to hose her legs when you're done? It must be pretty tough on her fetlocks, working in wet sand two days in a row."

"She's fine," Lynsey snapped. "Connemara ponies are hardy enough to cope with conditions that a more delicately bred horse like Bluegrass couldn't. They originated in Ireland, so they must be used to a little rain!"

Tell me something I don't know. Honey bit her lip. She

didn't want a showdown with Lynsey, who seemed to be on the edge of reason these days, ready to jump down everyone's throats. "I still think she's had enough."

"She's my horse, and I trust Lynsey to know what's best for her," Patience said crisply, now glaring at Honey.

Honey looked at the rain dripping off the ends of Minnie's mane. All she was doing by arguing with Lynsey and Patience was keeping the mare out even longer. "I'll leave you to it, then."

Patience gathered up the reins and looked expectantly at her, waiting for her to leave.

Honey sighed as she walked away from the arena. It was beginning to feel like her help wasn't needed anywhere.

On Monday morning Honey grabbed a muffin for breakfast and headed down to the stables before the start of classes. She hadn't gone to the barn the day before. The rain had poured until it looked like Dylan was going to turn into Mrs Noah after all, so the assistant housemothers had organized indoor games in the dorm. Just before dinner Honey had gone up to her room to fetch her jacket, in the hope of squeezing in a quick trip to the barn; but Lynsey was already there, pulling on her barn clothes. Honey had watched her and Patience run down the path to the barn with their coats held over their heads, feeling a certain brand of disappointment, knowing Minnie did not need her company. But Patience and Lynsey had appeared back in the Adams foyer about five minutes later, protesting about the mud that speckled their jeans and the way their hair always frizzed in the rain.

But at least they went down to check on Minnie, which is something, Honey thought as she walked into the barn the following morning. *They never come down before class, so there's no way I'll bump into them now,* she comforted herself as she pulled back the bolt on Minnie's door. Something told her Patience would be pretty angry if she thought Honey was still trying to check on her mare.

She jumped when she saw someone crouched down by Minnie's hind legs. Kelly, one of the stable hands, looked up as Minuet gave a low whicker. "Hi there."

Honey was tempted to draw back, to make it seem like she had entered the wrong stall. But she frowned when she saw the equine medical kit lying on the straw next to Kelly. "Is there something wrong with Minnie?"

Kelly fished a crepe bandage out of a bowl and squeezed out the excess water. "Easy, girl," she soothed as she began to wrap it around Minnie's hock. "Her legs are hot and swollen, so I'm putting on damp wraps," she explained to Honey. "They'll do a better job at cooling down the inflammation than dry ones. I noticed her looking uncomfortable when I came to give her breakfast, but I have no idea what she could have done. There's no evidence that she got herself pinned in the stall, because the straw would be a lot more mussed up, so the only other possibility is that she's been worked really hard. I'll have to check with Patience."

Honey went over to stroke Minnie's nose. As the mare's lip grazed her hand, Honey felt a rush of guilt. *This is my fault! I should have found a way to stop Patience from riding her on Saturday. I bet they didn't hose her legs after her workout, and they can't have checked her properly yesterday, either.*

"Can I help?" she asked, watching Kelly squeeze out a second bandage. The mare flinched in surprise and then stood quietly while Kelly wrapped it around her tendon.

"That would be great," Kelly said, without taking her eyes off what she was doing. "Can you do her forelegs? Keep in mind these are stable wraps, so they don't need to be as tight as exercise wraps, but they should still be pulled tighter against the bone than the tendon, especially since they'll loosen as they dry out."

With Kelly's OK, Honey came the rest of the way into the stall and rubbed Minnie gently between her eyes before reaching for one of the bandages in the bucket.

"It's OK," she murmured when Minnie shifted restlessly. Even through a layer of wet gauze, the mare's leg felt puffy and hot. Poor girl. "We're going to make you better, I promise," she said, tucking the end of the bandage in on itself.

She looked up at Kelly, who was packing up the medical kit. "Will she be better when we take these off?"

Kelly didn't answer for a minute. She ran her hand over Minnie's shoulder and pursed her lips. "It depends how bad the injury is. I'll let Ms Carmichael know what I've done, but I guess she'll want to call a vet to take a look. From what I can see, it looks like she's strained her tendons, which means she'll be off work for at least a few weeks."

Honey's heart sank. One thing was for sure: she wasn't going to let Patience intimidate her and keep her from caring for the mare. *Whether she and Lynsey like it or not, I'm going to do whatever I have to to make Minnie better.*

"Aren't you going to be late for class?" Kelly asked, looking at her watch.

Yikes! Honey had already missed the morning assembly, and English had started five minutes ago! She raced out of the barn, brushing white hairs from her blue kilt. Their English teacher, Ms Griffiths, was notorious for handing out detentions for the slightest transgression. She considered tardiness one of the seven deadly sins. She'd once given Alexandra a detention for turning up without her textbook, and that was only because Alex had been putting in extra study hours and had accidentally left it in the cafeteria!

Honey pounded across campus to the Liberal Arts building, feeling the cold air prick her face.

"I'm sorry I'm late!" she gasped, pushing open the door to the classroom.

Ms Griffiths looked up from her PowerPoint presentation on the theme of nature in *Macbeth*. "Take your seat, Honey. Dylan's already explained your absence."

As Honey walked to her seat, she mouthed her thanks to Dylan, wondering what excuse her friend had given.

"However, I don't consider going to see Mrs Herson about a broken bedside lamp a good enough reason for turning up late to my lesson," Ms Griffiths continued, answering Honey's unspoken question. "You could have used your break for that. So you can use your break to make up for what you've missed in my lesson instead. I'd like you to write an essay on Lady Macbeth's role in Macbeth's downfall."

"Yes, Ms Griffiths," Honey said, pulling her books out of her bag. She was aware of Lani's trying to catch her eye, but right now she didn't want her friend's –sympathy. She yanked the pages of her textbook over to find the scene that was being featured on the PowerPoint screen. A make-up essay? She was only ten minutes late!

Then she felt a stab of guilt. *How can I make a big deal out of a petty detention when Sam's at home trying to recover from chemo?* But no matter how hard she tried to tell herself to get a grip, Honey could feel her spirits plummeting. Nothing was going right.

Chapter Eight

Honey tightened Kingfisher's girth and led him out of his stall, ready for the Monday afternoon lesson. She had spent her whole lunch recess writing the essay for Ms Griffiths and hadn't had a chance to check on Minnie since that morning. She halted Kingfisher to look over the door at the grey mare, who was lying in a deep bed of straw.

"How are you doing, gorgeous girl?" she asked. Kingfisher snorted and nudged her shoulder. "Not you." Honey smiled, pulling out the tufty black forelock that was trapped underneath his brow band. "I'll come back later, I promise," she told Minnie, who hadn't taken her large dark eyes off Honey.

Honey halted Kingfisher as soon as they hit the yard and ran down the stirrups so she could mount. Once she was astride, she felt some of the tension run out of her. She clicked to the bay pony to walk on.

"You've come down in the world," Dylan joked, trotting up beside her on Morello.

"Shhh, he'll hear you." Honey leaned forward to cup

one gloved hand over Kingfisher's ear. "It's not his fault his legs aren't as long as Mischief Maker's."

"Yeah, right, because if you added four inches onto his height, he'd be every bit as talented at dressage." Dylan grinned.

Honey pretended to be insulted on behalf of the bright bay gelding, but Dylan's grin was infectious. Kingfisher was a good, steady jumper, even if he wasn't up to advanced-level dressage. "Don't worry, boy," Honey said, stroking Kingfisher's neck as they rode into the arena. "I still think you're great."

She was surprised to see jumps set out at one end of the arena. *I thought we were having a lesson on the flat.*

"Ms Carmichael's not able to take the class today, so she's asked me to stand in," Ms Phillips called from the centre of the arena. "I'd like you to start off by working without stirrups, please."

Honey concentrated on relaxing into Kingfisher's rhythm as he trotted around the ring, so she was part of his stride rather than bouncing around like a passenger.

"Good, Honey, you're moving with him perfectly," Ms Phillips praised. Honey felt a warm glow; she loved flatwork.

"OK, take back your stirrups," Ms Phillips called. She nodded toward the short course of fences at the bottom half of the arena. "I want you to jump the parallel, the wall, and then the stile coming out of the corner."

Dylan groaned.

"But we all know that Dylan and Morello don't do

corners," Lynsey explained, pointing out the low points of the pair's past performances as if she was trying to be helpful. Then Lynsey dropped her voice and glanced at Tybalt. After he didn't even make it through the practice round at the last show, she openly regarded him as a waste of effort. "But I guess that's better than not jumping *anything* well."

"Thank you, Lynsey. That's why we have riding classes," Ms Phillips commented evenly. "If everyone was perfect already, there'd be nothing to aim for. Perhaps you'd like to go first?"

Honey shook her head. Tybalt was overflowing with potential. It was just that he still had trouble focussing. Malory was the only one who had been able give him direction – and inspire him to work as part of a team. But Lynsey had little regard for process – only end product.

Honey watched as Lynsey shortened her stirrups and trotted Bluegrass around the jumps before he extended into a showy canter. She had to admit that they looked amazing. Every inch of Bluegrass's coat gleamed, even under the dark mane flowing away from his neck.

The blue roan gelding's stride didn't falter when Lynsey turned him at the parallel bars. He stood well back from the fence and launched powerfully into the air. As soon as he landed, Lynsey collected him and they cleared the wall effortlessly. Lynsey rode into the corner and turned him to face the stile. *Wrong leg!* Honey tensed, waiting for Lynsey to give Bluegrass the signal to change his lead. But before Lynsey reacted, Bluegrass was preparing to take off.

"Ouch!" Lani said, as the blue roan crashed through the narrow fence. "That must have hurt."

"Her pride, you mean?" Dylan asked as Lynsey trotted back to the group, looking flustered. "It's a good thing we've got you to show us how to do corners, Lynsey," she called.

Lani snorted with laughter as Lynsey glared at Dylan.

"That was a good example of when you should use the flying lead change," Ms Phillips explained. "Lynsey lost concentration and didn't have enough time to collect Bluegrass. On the correct lead, he would have had more balance for the takeoff."

Honey looked sideways at Lynsey, who was staring down at Bluegrass's mane. *That's not like Lynsey. She's usually at one hundred per cent. And Bluegrass could change leads in his sleep.*

"Right, let's have the other members of the junior team," Ms Phillips called. "Dylan, you're up next, then Malory."

Morello popped over the first two fences without a fuss, clearing the top rails with only inches to spare. *Why spend energy when you don't need to?* Honey thought in amusement. It was true that judges in huntseat classes preferred horses that did not overjump, but tackled the course evenly, conservatively. Honey's gaze followed Morello around the corner. She held her breath, hoping the paint gelding would make the sharp turn, and relaxed as Morello executed a textbook lead change and headed for the stile on the corrected leg. When they cleared the dauntingly narrow fence, the whole class burst into applause.

"So that's how you take the corner," Lani said loudly as Dylan cantered Morello back to join the group. "Thank you for the demonstration!"

I guess Lynsey asked for that, Honey thought.

When Tybalt headed for the first fence, Honey crossed her fingers. She really hoped the dark gelding would go well, knowing how much Malory wanted to take him to the All Schools League competition next week. *Come on, Tybalt.* At least he seemed to be having a good day; for once the shine on his coat was from a thorough brushing as opposed to a nervous sweat. It could be the handsome pony was coming around.

Malory rode Tybalt strongly at the first jump, and they flew over much more extravagantly than Morello had done. Honey noticed Malory's quick pat on his neck to tell him he'd done well before she sent him on to the second fence. Tybalt tucked his forelegs underneath him as he sailed over the bars; but when he landed, he tugged sharply against Malory's hands. Calmly Malory half halted the gelding to get him back under her control and then looked across at the stile. Honey could tell she was planning every stride, not letting Tybalt feel as if he was on his own for a single moment. *Go, Mal!* Honey felt a rush of delight when Tybalt cantered straight at the middle of the stile and took off at just the right moment. Even though his hooves rattled the top rail, it stayed up; and the class cheered when Tybalt landed clear.

"You know, Allbrights might have cleared a space in their trophy cabinet, but I can definitely picture that cup in the Chestnut Hill tack room at the end of the season," Ms Phillips declared, and the girls cheered even louder.

Paris Mackenzie went next on her own pony, Whisper. He rushed the first fence and brought it down. That squelched his overconfidence, and he jumped the next two carefully, going clear over them both.

"Well done," Ms Phillips called. "Honey, let's see what you can do."

Honey shortened her reins and cantered Kingfisher in a circle before turning him toward the parallel bars. She kept her legs on him until she felt him lift into the air, and felt a surge of pleasure when they landed clear. Picking up on her feelings, Kingfisher kicked up his heels. Honey sat deep in the saddle to bring his quarters under him before driving him on to the wall. Kingfisher hesitated, and Honey tapped him with her crop; but he took off too late. She groaned inwardly when the pony sent two of the top blocks flying with his forelegs. She concentrated hard on the last jump, determined to end on a good note. They were already on the right lead, just two strides away. *Yes!* Honey grinned as the bay landed without knocking the fence.

"Well ridden," said Ms Phillips, replacing the blocks on the wall before waving the next rider forward.

It was only when they were riding back to the barn that Honey realized that she hadn't thought of Sam once during the lesson. *Some twin I am*, she thought guiltily, leading Kingfisher into his stall. All of the pleasure of the lesson drained away; and when Honey rubbed Kingfisher down, she didn't chat to him as usual. *I'll call tonight for a progress report.*

She pulled Kingfisher's stable blanket into place before leaving him to munch from his hay net.

"Coming through!" Paris called as Honey stepped out into the aisle. She only just avoided colliding with Paris, who was half hidden under an armful of tack.

"Wait, you're dragging," Honey said, chasing after her and hooking the end of the reins over the saddle.

"Thanks," Paris said, her voice muffled as she pressed her chin against the riding hat perched on top of the saddle.

"Maybe two trips would have been better?" Honey suggested.

"Oh, you think?" Paris mumbled as she continued on down to the tack room.

Honey quickly headed for Minnie's stall but stopped short when she saw Patience adjusting one of the mare's bandages. She waited for Patience to kick in with the accusations when she saw Honey'd come to hang around Minnie again.

Patience looked up, and Honey noticed she had a bandage tangled around her hands like a bad knitting project. "I thought I'd take off her wraps to check her legs, but it's not as easy as it looks," she admitted, taking

Honey by surprise in a rare moment of candour.

"I'll give you a hand," Honey offered, stepping into the stall, relieved that at least this time Patience wasn't about to tell her to mind her own business. She knelt down and carefully unwound the rest of the bandage. She ran her hand down Minnie's leg and frowned when she could still feel some heat.

Lynsey peered over the door. "Oh, Honey. You're here again."

"Can you help me get the other bandage off?" Patience asked Lynsey.

"You're kidding, right?" Lynsey raised her eyebrows. "I've got hockey practice in like three minutes. It's hardly rocket science, taking bandages off. Anyone who owns a horse can do that, Patience – even you."

Whoa, that was harsh, even by Lynsey's standards. Honey caught sight of the blush flooding Patience's cheeks before she looked down so that her dark hair swung over her face.

"What did you tell Kelly about Minnie's legs?" Honey asked, wondering if Patience felt at all responsible for the mare's lameness.

"We just explained about her exercise schedule," Patience replied, sounding defensive. "Lynsey wants to bring Minuet to peak condition so she stands the best chance of making the junior jumping team."

"Well, she won't be good for any team if she's overworked," Honey pointed out, struggling to avoid sounding too judgmental as she took the last bandage off. "Is Kelly coming by to soak these and put them back on? I know she wants to try and keep the bandages cold and wet to help draw the heat out of Minnie's legs."

"I told her I'd do it," Patience said.

You couldn't take them off, how are you going to manage to put them on? Honey thought in disbelief.

"Will it take long?" Patience added.

"What?" Honey stared at her.

"I should go see if Lynsey's OK. You know she's helping organize the school auction as well. She's just got a lot going on." She stood up and patted Minnie's neck rather awkwardly. "You can finish up here, can't you?

Minuet snuffled at Patience's sleeve, leaving a wet smear. Patience pushed her nose away. "I have to call my dad, too, about a set of books he's donating for the auction. See you later." She let herself out of Minnie's stable without waiting to hear if Honey would stay and take care of her pony.

Honey bit down on a surge of anger as she went to fill a bucket with clean water. She didn't mind finishing Minnie's routine. She was angry that Patience couldn't see the benefits and responsibilities of horse ownership beyond looking good in the saddle, preferably a high-end Hermès saddle in a top class competition.

Minnie was standing awkwardly with her head hanging down when Honey got back to her. "You're feeling sorry for yourself, aren't you," Honey said softly, running her hand down the mare's neck. "I can't blame you. You deserve better."

Minnie sighed and rested her head on Honey's shoulder. Honey had never known a pony who appreciated human company the way Minnie did. "I'm going to visit every day so you don't get lonely," Honey promised. *I can't believe Patience is more interested in her friendship with Lynsey than taking care of you. That's the first indication that she's got her priorities wrong.* Honey soaked the bandages and began wrapping them around Minnie's legs. She was sure the tendons were more swollen than before. Honey took her time, amiably chatting and soothing the pony along the way. Once she was done, she straightened up. "That should make you feel a bit better," she told the mare, who whiffled at her pocket. "I'm going to go get you some extra straw for your bed."

As Honey left Minnie's stall, she noticed Dylan standing on the other side of the aisle. She was leaning over a stable door to stroke Nutmeg, the smallest pony on the yard.

"Hi there," Honey said, walking over. "She's so cute, isn't she?" Nutmeg was a favourite with all the students. Honey loved her thick bushy mane and the forelock that fell over her eyes.

"You sounded pretty chummy with Patience just now," Dylan said without looking at her.

"I did?" Honey was surprised by Dylan's frosty tone. Not only that, Patience had left several minutes ago. How long had Dylan been standing there? "I was helping her take Minnie's bandages off, that's all."

"Is that why you were late for class this morning?"

"Yes, I came down to check on Minnie and lost track of time," Honey admitted. "Thanks for covering for me."

Dylan shook her head, and Honey could tell her friend was close to being angry. "I can't believe I tried to cover for you when you were helping Patience. You know she was the one who got me into all that trouble and didn't have the guts to own up to it afterward! Why are you being so nice to her?"

"I told you," Honey snapped. Dylan was acting like Honey had been disloyal, but she hadn't asked Dylan to lie to Ms Griffiths for her! "I was helping Minnie."

Dylan turned to face her, green eyes blazing. "So basically you were only prepared to treat Patience like the traitor she is until she got herself a new horse. All you've done since Minnie arrived is hang around her stall. Are you hoping for a share?"

Honey took a step back. "It's not like that."

Dylan raised her eyebrows. "No? Well, what is it like?"

"I don't need to explain myself to you," Honey said, her heart pounding. "Why don't you just give me a break?"

"Yeah, whatever. You'll do whatever you want." Dylan turned on her heel.

Honey grabbed her arm. "And what's that supposed to mean?"

"It means," Dylan spun around, "that I'm starting to think you only look out for yourself. You act like you're one of the group, when the truth is you have your own agenda."

"My own agenda?"

"Come on, Honey. You are willing to hang out with anyone. Lynsey, Patience. And you kept secrets from us. I mean, I could understand Mal being closed off when she first arrived. She thought that if she told us she was on a scholarship, she wouldn't fit in. And it must have been really hard for her to come here so soon after her mom died. But there's not a single good reason I can think of why you didn't tell us you had a twin brother. We're supposed to be your friends! It just makes me wonder what other secrets you might be keeping from us."

"Oh, right, because the way you're acting really makes me want to tell you anything!" Honey took in a short, angry breath. In that instant she wanted to tell Dylan the truth about Sam. Then who would be casting accusations and placing blame? But Honey knew she couldn't use Sam's sickness to win some stupid fight. It was much too big for that.

Honey rubbed her forehead and tried to calm down. "Look, Dylan, I swear I wasn't thinking about Patience when I helped with Minnie. I was just trying to help a sick horse get better."

Dylan narrowed her eyes. "From where I'm standing, Minnie has plenty of people looking out for her – Kelly, Sarah, Ms Carmichael, Patience, Lynsey. Seems to me like her stall is pretty crowded already. Why would she need you?"

"Her stall looks pretty empty to me," Honey shot back, her cheek burning with anger. "If I hadn't gone in to check on Minnie just now, she wouldn't have had her legs wrapped tonight. Patience told Kelly she was going to do it, but she doesn't even know how."

"Are you suggesting Patience is clueless? Surely not!" Dylan said sarcastically. Her eyes were still smouldering, but the corner of her mouth twitched upward.

"It's a shocker. I never would have guessed." Honey forced a smile, feeling weak with relief that Dylan seemed to be over the worst of her temper.

Dylan glanced at her watch. "I'd better run," she said, her tone still somewhat cool. "I've still got that French homework to finish before tomorrow." She jogged down the aisle and vanished through the doors.

Honey crossed the aisle again to look inside Minuet's stall and leaned against the door. She knew Dylan had been hurt more than the others that she hadn't told them about Sam because they were roommates. Honey had a feeling that Dylan knew it had taken effort to keep Sam from everyone. But the hurt had obviously gone deeper than she'd thought. And now to make things worse, Dylan thought Honey was sucking up to Patience behind her back. *She obviously doesn't know me*, Honey thought, feeling a surge of indignation that just as quickly fizzled out. She didn't have the energy to fight with her friends.

"Why can't people be as straightforward as horses?" she sighed, leaning over the door to rub Minnie between her eyes.

* * *

After study period Honey went to the common room to listen to some music. She curled up on one of the sofas and closed her eyes, letting the latest Coldplay CD wash over her. After a while she was aware of Razina and Wei Lin setting a laptop down on the coffee table. Honey switched off her MP3 player and sat up to make room for them on the sofa.

Razina flipped open the laptop. "My mom offered to donate one of the pieces of jewellry from her last Kenyan trip to the auction. Which one do you think would be the biggest hit?"

Honey leaned forward to look at the screen as Razina began to click through the collection. "These are fabulous," she commented, as more and more colourful bracelets, necklaces, and earrings popped up.

"Your mother travels to all the villages to buy these things?" asked Wei Lin.

Razina nodded. "She's really into fair trade. She always employs a local interpreter so she can deal with the crafts–people directly. She's been dealing with some of them since before I was born."

Honey pointed at a necklace made out of dazzling beads in a dozen shades of green. "That one's gorgeous."

"It's a good-luck necklace," Razina said, clicking to enlarge the picture.

"If you get your mom to donate it, I can guarantee you at least one bidder," Honey told her. The necklace would make a perfect gift for her mother, who looked amazing in green – it brought out her holly-coloured eyes. Plus, her family needed all the luck they could get just now.

Wei Lin nodded. "It's really beautiful."

"OK," Razina agreed. "I'll get my mom to send it. It's great to think it might raise some money for the school library."

Honey caught sight of the time on the laptop display. It was getting late, and she hadn't phoned to check on Sam yet. She stood up. "I have to make a call."

"Catch you later," Razina said as Wei Lin waved.

Honey headed past the ping-pong table where Malory and Dylan were playing. "Honey, do you want to find Lani, and we'll play doubles?" Malory suggested with a smile. Dylan didn't look Honey's way.

"Sorry, I've got to go make a phone call," Honey said.

"OK, maybe later." Malory shrugged.

"Sure," Honey agreed. When she reached the door, she almost cannoned into Lynsey and Patience, who were standing just outside in the corridor.

"You knew I was planning to wear my wraparound skirt," Lynsey scolded. "Why did you go put on the same thing? I'm not going in there with us looking like Mary-Kate and Ashley. Can you go change?" She glared at Patience, who was wearing a Diane Von Furstenberg wraparound skirt with an identical pattern; but Lynsey's was lavender, and Patience's, ruby.

Looks like Lynsey is finding that having a clone has its drawbacks, Honey thought, hiding a grin as she dodged past. She wondered if she should tell Patience that she'd seen Ms Carmichael after she'd finished with

Minnie and found out that the vet was coming tomorrow. Before she had a chance to stop, Patience brushed past her on her way to the stairs, not even acknowledging her.

Honey walked along the corridor to the last bay window, which had a seat underneath. When she couldn't go outside, this was one of her favourite places in the dorm. It had a view that stretched down to the lawns in front of Old House, taking in the drive, the magnificent wrought-iron gates, and the edge of the stable yard. She pulled out her mobile phone to call home.

"Hi, Dad," she said when her father answered. She hesitated, knowing she'd promised not to call all the time to ask about Sam. *But do they really think I can just ignore what he's going through?* Asking her not to worry was like asking her not to breathe. "How's Sam?" she added.

"Well, the side effects of his chemo are kicking in, so he's not too good just now," her dad told her. "But we've been through this before, and the only thing we can do is help him ride it out. How did school go today?"

Honey could tell her dad was trying to change the subject. "Can I speak to him?" she asked.

"He's pretty drained. Maybe tomorrow," said Mr Harper. "I don't want you to worry, sweetheart. We're taking good care of him, I promise. How's the riding coming along?"

Honey's first thought was to tell him about Minnie,

but she bit back the words. *There's this wonderful horse who's really sick* wasn't exactly what her dad needed to hear right now.

"It's OK, thanks." What Honey really wanted were details about her brother. Didn't her parents know that the less they told her, the more her imagination went into overdrive? *If only Sam and I did have some kind of telepathy. It would make things a whole lot easier.*

"Why don't I get your mum so you can tell her all about your day?" Honey's dad said, putting down the receiver before she had a chance to say anything.

Honey leaned her head against the window's cold glass. Her parents were only trying to do the best for her and Sam. *But not being able to see Sam doesn't feel best. Why don't they see that?*

Chapter Nine

Ali Carmichael had arranged for the vet to visit the following afternoon. As soon as study hall was over, Honey raced down to the barn. She jogged breathlessly across the yard just as the veterinarian, Ms Olton, was getting into her SUV. Ms Carmichael was holding the gate open for her to back out.

"What did she say?" Honey called over the sound of the Jeep pulling away.

"Minnie's strained her tendons," Ms Carmichael replied. "She's been overworked, probably due to excessive schooling in the wet sand."

So it was the workout last Saturday that hurt her, Honey thought. She felt awful for Minnie. She was so generous. She only wanted to please people.

Patience and Lynsey arrived, looking irritated by the icy wind that whipped their hair around the faces.

"Has the vet been here?" Lynsey asked.

"Come into the barn, and I'll tell you what she said," said Ms Carmichael.

Lynsey glared at Honey when she followed them

into the barn, but Honey ignored her. She didn't care if Lynsey thought she was interfering. She wanted to know exactly what Minnie needed to make her better.

"The vet gave her a full inspection and says that she's strained her tendons," Ms Carmichael explained, stopping outside Minnie's stall.

Honey looked over the door. The mare was standing with her eyes half closed, dozing. "She's been given some bute to ease the pain," Ms Carmichael said, "but she'll need a lot of TLC to get her on the mend."

"When can she be ridden again?" Patience wanted to know.

"Not for at least two weeks," Ms Carmichael told her, pulling back the bolt on the door. "And then only if she recovers without any complications."

"There shouldn't be any – she's hardy enough," Lynsey said dismissively. "Two weeks is going to disrupt her training schedule as it is. She's going to lose muscle tone, and we'll have to really work to get her back in shape."

"Not if that work involves prolonged schooling in wet sand, you won't," Ms Carmichael said firmly.

Go, Ms Carmichael! Honey did a silent cheer for the Director of Riding, who seemed to know exactly who was responsible for Minuet's injury.

Lynsey didn't pick up on the warning note in Ms Carmichael's voice. "The junior team needs quality horses like Minnie if we're going to stand a serious chance of taking on Allbrights. Have you seen the breeding of their horses?"

"My focus at this moment in time is getting Minnie better. I'm surprised it's not yours," Ms Carmichael replied pointedly, transferring her gaze from Lynsey to Patience.

Honey struggled to swallow her anger. *Unbelievable! They damage Minnie's legs and now all Lynsey cares about is when Minnie'll be up and running again, like she's some kind of machine!*

"What does she need to make her better?" Patience asked.

"Obviously I'll supervise her care with Kelly and Sarah, but when I phoned your father to tell him about Minuet, he specifically asked that you take on some of the responsibilities," Ms Carmichael said. "We'll be glad to have you helping out, even if it's just in the evenings, since we're busy enough getting ready for the All Schools competition on Friday. You'll need to redo her bandages and make a warm bran mash to replace her hard feed."

"Warm bran?" Patience frowned. "Can't I just throw a handful into her regular feed?"

"The bran needs to be soaked in hot water, Patience. Since she's not going to be able to be out in the day, grazing, we need to make sure she's getting enough fibre," Ms Carmichael explained. "Giving her a bran mash is one of the best ways to keep her digestion working, especially since she's going to be on stall rest for a week. She can have short walks up the aisle to keep her from stiffening up, then we'll reassess her on Friday." Ms Carmichael ran her hand down Minnie's neck. The mare shifted her weight before beginning to doze again.

Honey couldn't understand why Patience hadn't gone into the stall to comfort Minnie. *Maybe she's just not as interested in Minnie if she can't ride her. But what will happen if Minnie doesn't get better quickly? Will Patience lose interest altogether?* Honey noticed Patience was picking at a splinter on the door, not even looking at her pony.

"I have to go. Hazel Goodfellow told me I've got to itemize the donations for the auction on Thursday night," Lynsey said, with a quick look at her watch. "If you're going to give me a hand, you have to be back in Adams in ten minutes," she added to Patience.

"Have Minnie's legs been wrapped for tonight?" Patience asked Ms Carmichael as Lynsey walked away.

Ms Carmichael nodded. "She just needs her mash, and a walk down the aisle."

"I don't mind doing it, if you've promised to help Lynsey," Honey said quickly.

Patience hesitated and bit her lip, then gave a quick nod. "Just for tonight, then," she said as she headed to the dorm.

"Don't do everything," Ms Carmichael warned when Honey stepped into the stall. Minuet nickered and pushed her nose into Honey's shoulder. "Patience has to take on some of the responsibility herself."

"I won't," Honey promised, scratching Minuet's forehead. "She's so sweet, it's no trouble."

"She has a lovely nature," Ms Carmichael agreed. "I'll

leave you to it, but I'll be in my office if you need me."

Honey decided to make the bran mash first, so it would have time to soak while she took Minnie out of her stall to stretch her legs. She boiled water in the kettle in the feed room and poured it onto the bran, inhaling the fragrant steam that rose out of the bucket.

Then she went back to the stall and buckled a halter onto Minnie's delicate head. "Come on, girl," she encouraged when the mare looked reluctant to move. "I know your legs hurt, but we won't go far, I promise."

Minnie let out a heavy sigh and kept her feet planted in her straw bed. "Come on, gorgeous," Honey encouraged. "You'll be fine, trust me." She rubbed her hand in small circles down Minnie's neck, the way she'd seen Malory do with Tybalt. "Just take your time," she told the mare.

When Honey clicked to Minnie to walk forward again, the mare took a hesitant step. "That's it," Honey praised, keeping the pressure on the lead rope. "Keep going, one step after another."

With painful slowness, Minnie followed her out of the stall. The mare laid her ears back when she stepped out of the straw and onto the concrete, but Honey urged her on, step by step, until they reached the top of the aisle. When they got back to the stall, Honey made a huge fuss over her. "You are so smart," she told Minnie. "And now I'm going to get you a yummy mash with chopped carrots, to make you feel really good."

As Minnie pushed her nose eagerly into the feed bucket, Honey smiled. She knew that with the right kind of TLC, the pony would soon be back in action. All she needed was time. *I just hope Patience is prepared to give it to you.*

Honey couldn't concentrate on any of her classes the next day. How could she get her head into a lesson on photosynthesis when there were things that seemed so much more important? She wasn't the only one who was restless. The school auction was scheduled for the next night, and the rumours about what was going under the hammer were getting wilder and wilder.

"Paris Mackenzie claimed that there's an O.C. script autographed by the entire cast." Taylor Goldberg, who was on the field hockey team with Lynsey, leaned across the aisle in history to whisper to Chantal Lafayette. "Some sophomore's dad is a talent agent in L.A., and he just had it lying around in his office."

"I heard there's a personally autographed pair of Brad Pitt's boxers up for grabs," Chantal whispered back.

Honey shook her head. What would anyone do with autographed boxers? The way the speculation was going, she wouldn't be surprised if a date with Elvis was going to be the final item up for bids.

Lynsey didn't even bother stopping for lunch in the student centre. Instead she managed to persuade the cafeteria staff to fix her a baguette and some fruit before she dashed off to call her mom's contacts whose donations for the auction hadn't arrived.

"It's a total nightmare," she ranted as she grabbed a

carton of juice. "There's a Ferrandis anklet that's magically disappeared into the ether. I mean, can anyone else explain how that could have happened, because I sure can't."

Honey wasn't sure why Lynsey had signed on for the auction on top of everything else. She didn't appear to have a second of free time, especially with the first official meet of the All Schools riding competition falling on the day after the benefit auction. Honey gave a mental shrug and carried her tray across to her favourite table. Patience was sitting at a table on her own, reading a magazine article. Honey was slightly surprised to see it was about Patience's dad. A colour photo of the Edward Hunter Duvall ranch was splashed across the centre of the page, with the author standing on a veranda, smiling into the camera with his trademark brighter-than-white smile.

Patience looked up as Honey walked by. "Thanks for the help yesterday."

"That's OK," Honey said, lingering at the end of the table. "How's Minnie today?"

"I don't know. I'll go down and see to her once Lynsey's tracked down the missing auction items," Patience said. "If she doesn't find out what's happened to that anklet she's going to have to take it out of the catalogue. The senior who is in charge is putting a ton of pressure on her. I'm just glad my dad's donation arrived a couple of days ago."

Honey hesitated. She could feel Dylan's eyes boring into her from the table behind her. *She probably thinks*

I'm sucking up to Patience again.

"Do you want to sit here?" Patience shifted her tray to make room.

"Um, thanks, but I think the others have saved a seat for me." Honey took a step toward her regular table.

Patience shrugged. "Whatever. Don't let me hold you up. You can't risk making yourself unpopular by hanging out with me, can you?"

"It's not like that." Honey felt awkward.

"Yes it is, it's exactly like that. All you and your friends have done since Thanksgiving is act like I'm America's Most Wanted. The truth is that it was Dylan who broke the rules when she rode Morello in the middle of the night. If I was so wrong to tell Mrs Herson what was going on, how come I never got punished? Don't answer that," she went on, holding up her hand. "We all know it's because the teachers thought I was acting responsibly."

Honey stared at her in disbelief. *Does she really think that made it acceptable to tattle on Dylan?*

"Like I said before, don't let me hold you up," Patience said coldly, tossing her head so her impeccably styled dark hair swung away from her face.

Honey was still seething over Patience's attitude when she sat down with the others.

"So, Honey, it looks like you're still playing both sides of the field." Dylan raised an eyebrow.

"What's the deal? Have you forgotten what she did to Dylan?" Lani added.

Honey felt her cheeks turning hot, even though she

127

knew she hadn't done anything wrong. Were they just teasing, or was it a serious accusation? "Forget what she did to Dylan? I don't think I could, considering it's thrown in my face every five minutes."

Malory looked from Dylan to Honey. "What's going on?"

"Don't ask Honey. You never get the whole story from her," Dylan said, getting closer to the truth than was comfortable.

Honey stared down at her plate. *While Dylan's getting angry over me saying two words to Patience, my brother's trying to fight off leukemia. It's all so pathetic.*

Suddenly Honey had had enough of being punished for caring about Minnie. She was just trying to help. "Why don't you just give it a rest, Dylan?" She shoved back her chair and glared at her friend. "It might amaze you to know that the world doesn't revolve around your feud with Patience. So I didn't tell you I had a twin — big deal. I didn't sign any contract when I came here, saying I had to declare my life history. Get over it!"

There was a stunned silence. Dylan's jaw was actually hanging open, and for one insane moment, Honey felt an urge to giggle.

Lani was the first to recover. "Um, I think I might have missed a major plot point. Since when did you guys declare war? I thought we were all on the same side. Us against them, you know. . ."

Honey didn't want to get into all this right now. "I'll catch you later," she said, getting up from the table and walking away. She wanted to blame Dylan, but a voice inside told her the fight was her fault. They'd been arguing about secrets, and she had done her best to keep her friends at a distance, as far from the truth as possible.

Honey walked out of the student centre and took in a deep breath of cold air. She decided to go down to check on Minnie. *Maybe Patience won't have time to go if Lynsey needs her help this evening,* she reasoned.

When Honey reached Minuet's stall, she found the mare lying down. Even when Honey pulled back the door and went in, Minnie didn't scramble to her feet. Honey crouched down by her head and stroked it gently. Minnie closed her eyes. She looked so vulnerable, lying there, and yet it was clear that she completely trusted Honey not to hurt her.

Honey reached out to touch one of the bandages. It was bone dry. "I'm going to fetch some clean water so I can change those for you," she murmured to Minnie.

The mare scrambled to her feet when Honey headed for the door. "It's OK. I'm coming back," she promised when the mare let out a low nicker.

She prepared another bran mash before filling a bucket with cold water. Minnie was still on her feet, looking over the door. "See, I promised I'd be right back," Honey told her.

Minnie stood quietly as Honey unwrapped the first bandage and soaked it in the water. Her legs were still hot, but Honey thought the swelling had gone down a little. *I wonder if she knows I'm trying to make her better.* Honey wouldn't have been surprised if the mare did. Minuet was a very intelligent pony.

She bandaged each leg in turn, pleased at the way Minnie stood as still as a rock for her. "You're such a good girl," she said, after finishing the last bandage. "I'm going to get your mash now. It should be cool enough."

"What on earth do you think you're doing?" Lynsey was glaring over the door at Honey, her blue eyes furious.

"I told you we'd be down after Lynsey had finished her calls," Patience protested from behind her friend. "You didn't even ask if you could come and do Minuet's bandages. You heard what Ms Carmichael said about my dad wanting me to help out. How am I supposed to take care of her if you do everything before I even show up?"

"Maybe that's the plan," Lynsey said, narrowing her eyes. "Was this Dylan's idea to get back at Patience? To keep her off the team by getting her pony taken away?"

"I'm not going to bother answering that," Honey retorted. "Don't worry about thanking me for helping out. I've done it enough times when you haven't bothered to stick around. And if I hadn't, she'd be a lot more ill than she is now."

"Is everything OK?" Ms Carmichael joined them. She didn't sound pleased to hear them arguing. "I'm not sure raised voices is something the vet prescribed."

"Everything's fine. We've just come to check on Minuet," Patience told her.

130

"That's good to hear," said Ms Carmichael. "Don't let me hold you up."

Honey gave Minnie's shoulder a quick pat before leaving the stall. "Her mash is ready in the feed room," she muttered over her shoulder before heading up the aisle. If looks could kill, she'd have been terminated under Lynsey and Patience's glares.

Ms Carmichael followed her. "You did her bandages tonight, didn't you?"

Honey hesitated, reluctant to get Patience into any trouble – after all, she hadn't given Patience much chance to get down to the barn first.

Ms Carmichael went on, "I saw Patience and Lynsey arrive several minutes after you, Honey. You have to give Patience the opportunity to look after Minuet herself, even though I know you must feel very frustrated that she doesn't seem as interested in her pony when she can't ride her."

This was so close to what Honey had been thinking that she stared at her riding instructor in surprise. Ms Carmichael raised her eyebrows. "On the other hand, the swelling in Minuet's legs is definitely going down, so I guess Patience should be grateful for your attention."

"I thought her legs were less swollen, too," Honey admitted. "She's such a sweet pony. I hate thinking of her shut in that stall all day."

"If her legs continue to improve, she shouldn't need much more stall rest," Ms Carmichael told her. "With any luck she'll be able to go back in the turnout paddocks next week, although I can't see she'll be fit enough to ride before the end of term." She pursed her lips and added, "I just hope Patience doesn't lose interest in her altogether." She collected herself and looked as if she regretted being so open in front of Honey.

Appreciating her instructor's candour, Honey said goodbye and jogged back up the path to the dorm. She just wished her parents could understand her need to be involved as much as Ms Carmichael did.

The following evening was the school auction to raise funds for the library. Lynsey and Patience went down to the gym early to check that everything was running according to plan. Knowing they wouldn't be free before the auction began for real, Honey went down to the barn to check on Minnie. After all, Ms Carmichael hadn't said she couldn't – she'd just said Honey had to give Patience a chance to look after Minnie first. She redid the soaked bandages, working quickly after several days' practice, before leading Minuet down the aisle for her daily stroll. She was delighted to see Minnie was walking less stiffly than before.

"It's a good start to the evening," she told the mare when she gave her the bran mash. Honey hadn't forgotten about the beautiful green necklace she wanted to buy for her mother. Minnie blew into her bucket like she was agreeing with her. Honey took it as another positive sign.

Honey ran back across campus to get changed for

the auction. Her room was empty, so she thought Dylan must have left ahead of her; but as she grabbed her purse, there was a knock on the door, and Lani looked in. "Ready?"

"You bet," Honey replied enthusiastically. She'd never been to an auction before, and she was really looking forward to this one. *Especially if I can get that necklace for Mum. It would be good to have a head start on Christmas shopping.*

Even though it was barely seven o'clock, the evening was dark and frosty. The Victorian-style wrought-iron lamp posts made the campus look like a scene from a Charles Dickens novel, and for a moment Honey had a pang of homesickness for London. She was distracted when Lani grabbed her arm and dragged her toward the gym, complaining she was so frozen she wouldn't be able to lift her arm to bid on anything.

They joined the line in the corridor to get into the gym, which spilled warm orange light from all its windows on to the students waiting outside. "Can you see anything?" Honey asked as Lani stood on tiptoe to peek through the open doors.

Lani shook her head. "There are too many people."

The line moved quickly, and Honey opened her purse to pay for the auction catalogue.

"Have a great evening. Spend lots of money. Let's get ourselves some great new books for the library!" Ms Marshall urged somewhat mechanically as she handed Honey her change and her bidding number.

"This should be fun," Lani enthused as they sat

down at one of the circular tables. Every table was covered in a chequered cloth with a small lamp in the middle. Most of the tables had filled up, but there were a few still empty in the middle of the gym. Honey and Lani sat down at one. "Seven," Lani said, quickly counting the chairs around the table. "Perfect."

Honey noticed Patience sitting close by at table three with Chantal and Taylor. She wondered if she should tell her that she'd taken care of Minuet already but decided against it. Patience might think Honey was trying to take over again, and she'd assume that Kelly or Sarah would deal with Minnie's bandages if she didn't go down to the barn.

Honey flipped open one of the notepads that had been put on each table and began sketching a pony's head on the front page. A pony with large dark eyes and a broad, well-shaped head.

"Hey, check out page six, there really is an O.C. script signed by the whole cast!" Chantal exclaimed from table three.

Honey and Lani began thumbing through their catalogues. "Wow," Lani said. "She's right. This is going to be some night. I predict a fight among our pals on the left."

Honey grinned. Chantal and Taylor were already arguing over how much they'd bid to get their hands on the script.

"But what I really want to know is if there's going to be any fighting at table six," Lani said.

Number six was their table. Honey winced at the

serious note in Lani's voice, and guessed she was talking about her argument with Dylan. "We'll behave ourselves, I promise," she said.

"Why was Dylan so mad at you?" Lani asked, frowning. "I know she feels that your helping out with Minnie is giving Patience the message that she's been for–given. But I get the feeling there's something more to it than that."

"I don't know," Honey said, looking down.

"Maybe she figures you're still holding out on us," Lani speculated. "I think she needs more juicy details on that twin of yours. I could use some, too."

Honey shifted uncomfortably. *Since when had her friend become psychic?* And the irony was that Honey was still keeping secrets, though Dylan didn't know it. Lani's tone was light enough, but Honey didn't have the energy to laugh off the mention of Sam. "I don't know what you mean."

Lani's expression turned serious. "Come on, Honey. You're not concentrating in class, you're so pale you look like you've stepped out of *The Blair Witch Project*, and you even managed to get yourself a detention, which has to be a first in your entire lifetime. Maybe I should ask Minnie what's wrong, since you seem to spend more time with her than with us!"

Honey's fingers tightened around her catalogue. "So I talk to a horse. I've heard you chatting to Colourado often enough."

"Guilty as charged." Lani grinned. "So are you telling me everything's OK, or are you telling me to keep my nose out of your business?" She reached out and put her hand on Honey's arm.

"Whose business?" Dylan asked as she and Malory arrived.

"Honey's," Lani told her.

Honey tensed, waiting for a biting comment about keeping secrets from Dylan.

To her relief Dylan just said lightly, "Well, you might as well cut your losses. Honey could be in the Mafia with all the secrets she keeps!"

As the others laughed, Dylan slid onto the chair alongside Honey. "Hey there," she said, more quietly.

"Hey there," Honey said carefully.

Dylan sighed and drummed her fingers on her catalogue. "I think I owe you an apology. You were right. It's up to you to decide what you want to share with the rest of us. Maybe I'm just jealous because the closest thing I have to a brother is my dorky cousin."

"Whoa! If you're talking about the gorgeous Nat, then give me a dork any day," Lani teased, overhearing them.

Honey wasn't ready to let the moment go just yet. "Thanks," she said, lifting her eyes to look at Dylan. "I guess I should appreciate having friends who care enough to worry." But part of her wished Dylan wasn't being so understanding. It just made Honey feel even worse to know she was still holding something back.

Razina, Wei Lin, and Alex arrived together.

"Have you decided what you're bidding on?" Razina asked, putting her stick with the bidding number attached to it down on the table.

"Oh, only every single item," Lani replied. "Have you seen some of the stuff in here?"

"Well, you can all keep your hands off the set of signed books Patience's dad donated," Wei Lin said, sounding deadly serious. "I've already cleared a space for them on the shelves above my bed."

"Isn't the whole idea that we bid against one another to raise money?" Malory pointed out as the overhead lights dimmed, leaving each table lit by their individual lamps. Ms Keeler, the librarian, walked onto the stage. She'd agreed to kick off the auction.

"What a fantastic turnout!" Ms Keeler enthused, beaming down at the tables of students. "I'm not going to add a boring note to this evening by ranting about school resources."

Somebody toward the back of the room cheered.

"But," Ms Keeler continued, smiling, "I will just say that I've cleared an entire section in the library, confident that tonight's auction is going to do a great job of filling the empty shelves. Now I'm going to hand over the stage to one of your student reps, who has put so much hard work into organizing tonight's event: Hazel Goodfellow."

Hazel, one of the senior student council reps, smiled at Ms Keeler as they passed one another on the stage. Lynsey followed Hazel onto the platform and stood near to the wing, ready to hold up each item when the bidding started. As usual, she looked like she'd walked straight off the pages of *Vogue*. Her bejewelled Jimmy

Choo sandals, paired with a black wool shift, would have looked like overkill on anyone else, but on Lynsey the outfit just made everyone else feel underdressed. Honey smoothed out a wrinkle on her flared skirt, wishing she'd teamed it with her suede boots.

"The student council has asked me to thank you all for coming." Hazel flashed a professional smile. "Let's have a great night and raise lots of money for the library!"

Honey picked up the jug of sparkling water that had been placed on the table and began filling everyone's glasses. She was waiting for Lot Three, the good-luck necklace.

The bids began to fly around the room for the first lot, a brand-new electric guitar donated by Faith Holby-Travis's father, who owned a chain of music stores. To everyone's surprise, Dylan lifted her bidding stick.

"Since when do you play guitar?" Malory whispered.

Brooke Peterson, president of the student body, raised the bid by twenty dollars, and Dylan waved her number again. "I've always wanted to learn," she explained out of the corner of her mouth.

"You'll be out of money by the second lot if you're going to bid for everything," Wei Lin warned.

"It can get totally addictive – I recommend sitting on your hands," Razina warned, her dark eyes dancing. "I've been to a couple of auctions with my mom, and believe me, people can end up paying way over the value for stuff they wouldn't look twice at in a store."

"Yes, but it's for a good cause, isn't it?" Lani pointed out.

"One hundred and eighty dollars going once, going twice. . ." Hazel paused, looking around the gym. "Sold!" She banged down her gavel on the podium. "To number eighty-three."

"Yay!" Dylan waved her bidding stick jubilantly in the air.

"Great, now all you need is one hundred and eighty lessons to learn how to play," Lani said dryly.

Honey picked up her number, ready to start putting in bids for the necklace after Lot Two, a health spa voucher, went quickly. The bidding for the necklace started at ten dollars. Honey began to raise her stick, and Lani leaned across. "You need a strategy. Jump in later on, just as someone thinks they're about to get it. I learned that tactic watching a TV auction."

Honey hesitated, torn between jumping in and taking Lani's advice. Delaney Foster, the correspondent from Walker House for the school paper, had already pushed the bidding up to twenty-two dollars against Eleanor Dixon and Sara Chappell. At thirty dollars Eleanor dropped out. Honey's fingers tightened around her bidding stick.

"Not yet," Lani murmured. The bidding stalled at thirty-eight dollars until Delaney raised her stick to bid forty.

"Now!" Lani said. "And act like you're prepared to spend hundreds."

"Forty-five dollars," Honey called out, lifting her stick.

Sara and Delaney both looked over at her in surprise.

"Any advance on forty-five?" Hazel asked. She raised her hammer as Sara shook her head.

"Forty-seven," Delaney said.

"Go on, she's all done in," Lani said confidently.

"Fifty dollars," Honey called, knowing that was her whole allowance. It was worth it; the necklace looked even prettier under the lights on the stage. She knew her mom would love it.

Delaney shook her head and put her stick back down on her table.

"Going once, going twice. . ." Hazel paused.

Hurry up!

"Sold!" Hazel announced, dropping her hammer. "To number fifty-two."

Honey sat back in her chair, feeling a rush of delight. She couldn't wait to see her mom's face when she opened her gift.

"Check out Lot Seven. It's a rugby shirt signed by the British Lions team. Honey, you didn't donate that, did you?" Razina asked, looking up from her catalogue.

Honey shook her head, feeling disappointment wrench at the pit of her stomach. She hadn't even seen it in the listings. *Sam would have loved that shirt. I can't believe I just spent all my money on the necklace. What was I thinking?*

"Honey."

She jumped as someone touched her shoulder.

Mrs Herson bent down to speak into her ear. "I'm sorry to drag you away, but there's a phone call for you in my office. It's your mom. She said she's been trying to call your mobile, but it's turned off."

Honey dropped her bidding stick and shoved back her chair, her pulse racing. Sam! Something must be wrong. As she sprinted across the lawn, she fumbled for her mobile phone and switched it on. A message flashed on screen showing four voice mails. Her mom had obviously tried to phone her several times. *This is why I should be at home. Why am I at a stupid auction when I'm needed there?*

Honey ran up the stairs to Mrs Herson's office and scooped up the receiver. "Mum? What's wrong?"

"We've had to take Sam back to hospital." Mrs Harper got straight to the point. "He's had a bad reaction to the chemo, so they want to keep an eye on him."

"What do you mean, a bad reaction? What's happening to him?" Honey could hear the panic in her voice as she almost shouted into the phone.

"Calm down, sweetheart. I didn't mean to scare you. It's nothing that the hospital can't handle. They're running some tests on him now."

Honey forced herself to take a deep breath. "What's wrong with him, Mum?"

"He's vomiting a lot, and his temperature's sky high. They need to put him on a drip to rehydrate him and bring down the fever," her mother admitted.

Honey's legs suddenly gave out, and she had to grip Mrs Herson's desk to stay upright. "I want to see him." Her voice sounded croaky, and she coughed.

"You can, I promise. Soon. Right now your being here wouldn't make any difference. It's better if you stay at school, and maybe you can visit in a week or so, if he's better."

Honey felt stunned. Her mom knew how close she and Sam were. Just because Honey didn't have a magic wand to wave to make him better didn't keep her from needing to be with him.

"I'll phone back and explain what's going on to Mrs Herson," Mrs Harper went on. "I just made a quick trip home to pick up some fresh pyjamas for Sam. I know this is hard, but try not to worry. I love you, sweetheart."

Honey couldn't answer as her mom hung up. All her worst nightmares were coming true. *What if Sam thinks I don't want to go to the trouble to see him? If Mum doesn't tell him she wouldn't let me come, then he'll think I don't care.*

Chapter Ten

Honey woke early and couldn't get back to sleep, even though her alarm clock showed it was only five-thirty. In the end she gave up trying and got out of bed. She grabbed her jeans and a hoodie and went to the bathroom to get dressed. The last thing she wanted was to wake Dylan and Lynsey. They'd had a late night with the auction, and today they were jumping in their first competition in the All Schools League.

Honey bit her lip as she looked at her reflection in the mirror. Lani had been right; she did look pale. She reached for a makeup brush and swept some blusher along her cheekbones. *Great! Now I look like I've got a rash or something.* She grabbed a towel and rubbed the blusher off but decided to leave her hair down. At least having it swinging over her face went some way toward disguising the fact that she wasn't looking her best.

Honey slipped out of the dorm, using her electronic pass to get out of the main doors in the foyer. It wasn't completely light yet, but she loved how peaceful the campus felt with no one else around. The trees still had a few coppery leaves clinging to their branches, although most of them had fallen to form crisp beds of red, gold, and amber. She walked across the broad sweep of lawn below Old House, inhaling the scent of wood smoke and rain as she followed the track that led down to the lake. Pale fronds of mist hung over the top of the water. It was like a scene out of King Arthur; Honey half expected the Lady of the Lake to break the surface, holding Excalibur in her slender white arm.

She thought back to the holiday she and Sam had taken with their parents near Tintagel in Cornwall in southwest England. King Arthur was supposed to have been born there, in a craggy stone castle that rose out of a wild, windswept cliff. There had been a medieval weekend in the village when they'd arrived, and she and Sam had tried out the archery. Honey grinned. She'd been useless! At one point one of the instructors had asked her if she'd deliberately aimed at the tents set up outside the shooting ring. Of course, Sam had been amazing, even though he'd never held a bow before. In no time at all, he was landing his arrows in the centre of the brightly painted target. Honey could still picture his face, even more freckled because of the sun, laughing with sheer delight as he hit the bull's-eye for the first time.

They could never have guessed it was the last holiday they'd have together before Sam was diagnosed with leukemia.

Honey gasped out loud as she recalled the moment she'd been told her twin was seriously ill. She'd completely fallen apart for the first few days, unable to sleep or eat or do anything but cry. Sometimes she wondered if that was the reason why her parents had sent her to Chestnut Hill. They couldn't have known Sam would get sick again. At the start of term, he had still been heading toward remission – but perhaps they'd been afraid that if he regressed, Honey wouldn't be able to cope.

She pulled her coat closer against the cold morning air and listened to the distant splashes of ducks leaving the island in the middle of the lake. It was getting light, and Honey figured the stable staff would be getting the horses ready for the competition by now.

She made her way across to the yard, smiling at the sound of whinnies carried on the breeze as the horses demanded their breakfast. When she got into the barn, the horses were all looking over their doors with their ears pricked, watching Sarah going from stall to stall with buckets of feed.

"You're up early," Sarah greeted her.

"I thought I'd check on Minnie before the rush," Honey explained.

"Before the stampede to get the horses ready for the competition, you mean?" Sarah grinned.

Honey nodded. "I promised I'd help Malory with Tybalt." After their strong performance in lessons and practice this week, Ms Carmichael had agreed to let Malory ride the dark brown gelding in the team's first official competition. Malory hadn't stopped smiling for forty-eight hours straight – Lani swore she'd even been grinning in her sleep.

"We'll need all the help we can get with all three of the teams travelling," said Sarah. "Do you want to take Minnie's breakfast to her?"

"Sure." Honey carried the feed into the stall. The grey mare whickered loudly and rustled through the straw toward her. "Hungry?" Honey smiled, setting the bucket in its holder on the wall.

Minnie thrust her head into the bucket and began to munch.

"She's enjoying that," Ms Carmichael commented, looking over the door.

Honey nodded.

"I'd hoped Patience would be here to check on her this morning. I wanted her to take a look at Minnie's legs," Ms Carmichael said.

"Why, what's wrong?" Honey asked, feeling a flash of panic. She crouched down, making sure Minnie didn't mind being touched while she was eating, and quickly unwrapped a bandage. She ran her hand from her knee to her slender fetlock. The skin was cool beneath Honey's fingers, and she could feel the smooth, hard bone clearly through the skin. There was no swelling left at all.

"She's better?" Honey stared at Ms Carmichael, hardly able to believe that Minnie had recovered so quickly. "Just like that?"

"Well, I'm not sure we can say 'just like that.' It's thanks to several days of soaked bandages, stall rest, and some excellent company," Ms Carmichael said. "I'd hoped to congratulate Patience, but I get the feeling I'm looking at the one who is responsible."

Honey felt herself turn red. She knew that Mr Duvall had specifically asked for Patience to look after Minnie. *But I couldn't turn my back on Minnie when Patience didn't come through for her.*

Ms Carmichael allowed the silence to drag out before saying, "She's going to need very gentle exercise for the next few weeks, starting with being turned out for a couple of hours this afternoon and then maybe a couple of circuits in the arena tomorrow. She can't be ridden for a while, but the important thing is that she's over the first hurdle. All she needs is a bit of patience – or perhaps I should say a lot more of Patience. It really is important that she involves herself in Minnie's recovery, and I'll be telling her so when I see her. I appreciate your dedication, but you need to let Patience care for her pony."

Honey nodded. She was thrilled at the thought of Minnie returning to work, even though Ms Carmichael was obviously not pleased that she had been Minnie's primary caregiver instead of her real owner.

But Honey was not going to make excuses. Minnie had needed her, and she had helped the pony. Honey hugged the grey mare in delight. *I'll have to email Sam and let him know*, she thought. Then her excitement evaporated. Sam was too sick to check his emails or answer the phone.

As soon as Ms Carmichael left, Honey took off the remaining three bandages. "Lynsey was right about one thing," Honey told Minuet when she reached the final leg. "You are pretty strong after all." Minnie stretched her head around to snuffle her hair, and Honey laughed. "You're healing nicely. Just don't go running around in the paddock. We can't let you undo all this work. I like having you in one piece!"

She left Minnie to rest while she went to give a hand with the mucking out. By the time the clock in the tack room showed seven-thirty, the members of the three riding teams, junior, middle school, and senior, were arriving to start grooming.

"Can someone get me a hoof pick for Skylark?" Eleanor Dixon yelled, sounding way more stressed than the junior team captain usually did on a show day.

Honey ducked into the tack room and rummaged around in a grooming box.

"I thought I'd find you here," Lani said, appearing in the doorway. "What happened to you last night?"

Honey spun around, feeling her cheeks flush guiltily. "What do you mean?"

"Oh, come on, Honey. We were all having a great time at the auction. Then Hersie appears, says something to you, and you disappear for the rest of the night. What's going on?"

"Nothing. I had to take a call in her office, and by the time it was finished, there wasn't much point in coming back." Honey knew it was a lame excuse, but she didn't feel like coming up with an elaborate lie to cover her tracks.

Lani's eyebrows shot up. "How long was the call? What's going on, Honey? I know something's been bugging you, and if you tell me nothing again, I'll make you eat that hoof pick."

Honey looked down at the metal pick. It didn't look appetizing, nor was the thought of ruining everyone's day by telling them the truth about Sam.

"I thought we were friends," Lani said quietly. Her words felt like thorns.

"We are." Honey looked up, meeting Lani's gaze.

"Then you should act like you believe it. All we want to do is help you, but it's like you have this brick wall around you."

"You can't help." Honey shook her head, feeling a lump rise in her throat. There was no way she was going to cry. If anyone had the right to cry, it was Sam, not her.

"How do you know if you don't give us the chance?" Lani persisted.

Honey swallowed hard. "Trust me, Lani, you can't."

"Try me." Lani came into the tack room and put her hand on Honey's arm. "I can plot my way out of any problem. And if that doesn't work, pleading comes in handy, too."

"Can you find a cure for leukemia?" The words came out in a rush, before Honey had a chance to think about what she was saying, and she gazed at Lani in horror. *What did I say?*

Lani stared back at her. "What do you mean? Who has leukemia?"

Honey sighed. Well, that was it. She knew she couldn't keep it in anymore.

"Sam," she said hoarsely. "It's come back, Lani. We thought he was in remission, but it's back." She took a deep breath, realizing that she wasn't telling it properly. "Sam fell ill two years ago, when we were still living in England. I gave him some of my bone marrow for a transplant, and he went into remission. When we moved out here, he wasn't healthy enough to go to school, but he'd planned to go to Saint Kits in the New Year, with my mum home-schooling him until then." Her voice wobbled as she tried to get the next sentence out. "When I went home for Thanksgiving, they told me the cancer had come back. That phone call I got last night was from my mum to say that he had a bad reaction to his chemo so he's been taken to the hospital. I asked if I could see him, but she said he needs to rest."

Lani raked her hand through her hair. "Oh, gosh, Honey. I'm so sorry. Why didn't you say anything? This explains so much."

"I couldn't. I mean, I can't talk about it. I can't even see him," Honey whispered, still trying desperately not to cry. "Mum told me I might be able to visit next weekend."

"But that's forever from now!" Lani exclaimed, her face etched with concern.

Honey shot her friend a look. *Thanks, Lani. I kind of knew that already.*

"Why can't you go see him today?"

Honey shook her head. "Sam's too sick for visitors right now."

"You're not a visitor. You're his sister!" Lani exclaimed.

"I know," Honey said tightly, "but my parents know how much Sam can take. I have to trust their decision."

"All your parents can see is Sam. They can't see you being eaten up by what's going on. But I can. It's obvious how hard this is on you. I think you should call them and ask them to come pick you up. Even if they don't think it will make Sam better, tell them it would do you a world of good. Sam isn't their only child, and they don't love him more than they love you. They just don't have a clue how much you need to see him."

Honey stared at Lani. She'd never let herself think that way before. She'd just gone with what her parents thought was the best for Sam. *But maybe he needs to see me as much as I need to be with him.*

Before Honey could say anything, Lani was heading for the door. "I have to go. I promised Dylan I'd help her with Morello. But I'm not going to forget this. I'll help you figure it out. Oh, and Honey?" She looked back over her shoulder. "I know it must have been hard telling me about Sam. But I'm glad you did – and that you don't have to deal with it on your own anymore."

"I'm glad, too," Honey said honestly. "I should have told you before." Nothing was going to make her stop worrying about Sam, but Lani was right; it wasn't something she had to deal with on her own now. *That's the thing about friends; they're there for you through the good times and the bad. I should have trusted them to know how to handle the news about Sam right from the start.*

Fishing her mobile phone out of her pocket, Honey called her mom. Lani had to be right, didn't she? If she could explain how important it was that she see Sam, her mom would come get her at once. Honey pressed the phone close to her ear, rehearsing what she'd say. Her heart sank when she was forwarded straight to voice mail. "Mum, it's me. I've been thinking about how far away next weekend is, and I really don't want to wait that long to see Sam. Can you come pick me up? I know you said I should wait until he's better, but this is really important to me. Please. Call me back as soon as you get this, OK?" She hesitated. "And tell Sam I love him."

Honey took the grooming kit down to Tybalt's stall and propped her phone on the partition with the volume turned up loud so she wouldn't miss her mom's call if she picked up her voice mail.

"Morning. Where did you run off to last night?" Malory paused while she cleaned the body brush against a currycomb.

"Don't ask! Long, long phone call." Honey had no intention of telling Malory and Dylan what was going on with Sam right before the competition. They needed their total concentration on the horses, particularly Malory, who was still in need of a lot of reassurance when it came to Tybalt's reliability. Talking to Lani had put things in perspective. Honey would tell Malory and Dylan the truth at some point, just not before their big event.

Malory didn't push the issue. As she started

brushing Tybalt's quarters, she dropped the currycomb into the straw. "That's the third time I've done that."

"Nervous?" Honey asked sympathetically.

"Is it that obvious?" Malory forced a smile. "I just want Tybalt to do his best. Not for me, but for him. He's worked so hard these last few weeks, and I don't want anything to mess up his chances. This could be his last shot to prove that he really belongs here."

"You've both worked hard," Honey reminded her. "And you both deserve a second chance. I think that's how you should view it. A second chance, not Tybalt's last." She began twisting braiding bands around sections of Tybalt's glossy black mane.

Malory smiled again, this time a little more convincingly. "That's a good way to think of it," she said. "Of course I'm still keeping my fingers and toes crossed that he's not going to get spooked by anything today."

"Just keep him clear of other horses," Honey warned, remembering how a near collision with Caleb's horse at the last competition had freaked Tybalt out. "Have you heard from Caleb lately?"

"He's emailed a few times," Malory admitted, running a stable rubber over Tybalt, even though his dark brown coat was already gleaming. "Nothing too mushy, just stuff like asking me if I'm nervous about the show."

"You're not giving out inside information are you?" Honey teased.

"Nope, although Caleb did try and get some

information out of me," Malory said mysteriously. "Except it wasn't about the team. He wanted to know about you."

"Me?" Honey said in surprise.

"His friend Josh has been asking about you," Malory told her. "He wanted to know if the call you got in the coffee shop was from your boyfriend. I hope you don't mind, but I told Caleb it was from your twin brother."

"That's OK, I guess," Honey said uncertainly. Josh had been cute, but right now dating was the last thing on her mind. She finished the last braid. "Tybalt's going to outclass every horse there, even the legendary Bluegrass."

"That's not allowed. I'm sure it's written in some rule book somewhere that Bluegrass has to come out on top," Malory joked.

"Wow, Tybalt looks terrific," Lani whistled, leaning over the stall door. "If it was a beauty competition, you'd have it in the bag."

"You mean you don't think we do anyway? Some cheering squad you're going to be," Malory teased.

"Oh, I'll be cheering loud enough for two people," Lani said, looking at Honey.

"That's what we like to hear, right Tybalt?" Malory patted the showy gelding and beamed at her friends.

"I'll start taking stuff off the trailer," Lani offered. "Can you help me with the tack, Honey?"

Honey nodded and followed her down the aisle, dodging to avoid Eleanor Dixon and Olivia Buckley, who were leading Skylark and Shamrock out to the trailer. Both the bright chestnut mare and the blue-grey gelding were gleaming, their hooves glistening with oil and their leather halters polished to perfection. Honey thought back to the last horse show at Saint Kits, where she had been as fired up and sleepless as the members of the team. This time it was like watching everything through a pane of glass – like everything was happening around her, but she just couldn't join in.

"Did your mom agree to pick you up?" Lani whispered as they collected two sets of saddles and bridles from the tack room.

Honey shook her head. "Her phone's off, which would make sense if she's in the hospital. She might check her messages later and call me then."

"OK, we can see if she gets back to you while we're on our way to Allbrights," Lani said. "But if she doesn't, we'll have to switch to Plan B."

"Plan B?" Honey frowned. "Have I missed something?"

"Didn't I tell you I could plot, plan, or plead my way out of any situation?" Lani grinned. "You're going to see Sam today. I guarantee it!"

Chapter Eleven

"How?" Honey grabbed Lani's arm after they had loaded the tack into the trailer and pulled her into an empty stall. "How can you know for sure?"

Lani pressed a finger to her lips. "We're going to be at Allbrights all day, right? And that's on the other side of Cheney Falls, closer to the hospital than we are here. If you disappear for a few hours, no one's going to notice."

"You mean I'm not going to wait for my mum to pick me up?"

"If she's spending the day at the hospital, she might not get your call until tonight."

Honey felt her stomach twist with excitement. The way she was feeling right now, she'd do anything to get to Sam.

"I'll cover for you," Lani promised. "Since every team is competing, we'll be taking all three school trailers plus the minibus. There'll be students all over the show ground – no one's going to notice if you're not around. All you have to do is make sure you're back here at about the same time as we are. Just don't stay too long and miss dinner. It's pizza tonight!"

"What are you, my lifestyle coach?" Honey said, her mind racing with the possibility that she might be with Sam in just a few hours. *What did I do to deserve friends like this?* Impulsively she leaned forward and gave Lani a hug. She pushed away the small voice in her head that said how much trouble she'd be in if she got caught. She knew if the roles had been reversed, Sam would have done this for her without thinking twice. He'd always been the daring, impulsive one.

"I can't believe you've thought all this out. You sound like you do this kind of thing all the time!"

Lani looked a little guilty. "I *have* done something like this once. My family had just moved to Colourado Springs, and I really missed my friends back in Washington. My parents wouldn't allow me to go back for a visit." She pulled a face. "They thought that if I saw them so soon after moving, it would make it even harder for me to settle in. I decided they were way out of line, so I worked out one of my amazing plans." She waggled her eyebrows, and Honey couldn't help giggling. "I left school at lunch and got on a Greyhound heading east. I only made it to the next town, because a co-worker of Dad's spotted me from her car at a traffic light. She flagged the bus down and made me get off before driving me home. My parents lectured me, but they also finally realized how homesick I had been."

"You'd really click with Sam, he's like that, too," said Honey. "I was always the sensible twin. While he was climbing the highest tree on our street, I'd be piling coats on the ground in case he fell. "

"You should do that more," Lani told her.

"What?"

"Talk about Sam. It's obvious he means so much to you. I can't believe you managed not to mention him all term!"

Honey shrugged. She knew how hard it had been – and how she had probably wasted all that effort. She reached out and squeezed her friend's hand. "Thanks, Lani. I won't forget this."

"Don't worry." Lani gave her a quick smile. "I have no intention of letting you. So you know what you've got to do? If your mom doesn't call you to say they're coming by the time we reach Allbrights, then you'll catch a bus to the hospital yourself. I'll make sure that everyone thinks you're at the show ground while you go see Sam. And as long as you get back here by the time we all show up, then no one's going to suspect a thing."

"OK," said Honey, squaring her shoulders. She hoped the plan was as foolproof as Lani made it sound.

"Steady, Tybalt," Malory soothed when the dark gelding clattered off the ramp onto the busy show ground.

Honey didn't like the way Tybalt's nostrils were flaring as he held his head high, looking all around.

"Is there any chance of getting Blue unloaded sometime today?" Lynsey called from the top of the ramp. Patience was alongside her, holding Bluegrass's tack.

Honey took hold of the other side of Tybalt's halter and helped Malory walk him around to the side of the truck. Once he was tied up, Malory began working her hands in small circles down the gelding's neck. Honey watched the T-touch take effect as Tybalt lowered his head, his ears going floppy.

"He looks like he's going to be fine," Honey said softly.

Malory smiled, but Honey recognized the strain on her face. It was exactly how she had been feeling herself, ever since Thanksgiving break.

Dylan and Lani led Morello off the ramp and tethered him next to Tybalt. It was great to see the way the stylish bay stretched out his nose to say hello to the paint pony. One of Tybalt's biggest difficulties after arriving at Chestnut Hill had been socializing with other horses. Now he seemed to have got over the worst of his demons, thanks to Malory's patience and the vet student Amy Fleming's great advice.

"Don't wait too long before you start warming Tybalt up," Ms Phillips warned, bringing the ponies' tack out from the truck. "He needs plenty of time to relax."

Malory nodded as she bent down to strap on Tybalt's galloping boots.

"We'll go get some drinks," Lani said, looking at Honey and nodding her head slightly.

Honey's stomach flipped over. Her mom hadn't

called, even though she'd checked her phone every couple of minutes. It was time for Plan B!

"Two coffees for Ms Carmichael and me, please. She's helping the seniors unload," Ms Phillips said.

"No problem. There's a bit of a line over at the concession stand so it might be a while," Lani answered.

Honey took a deep breath. *This is it.* "You guys are going to be great. You know I'll be rooting for you." She still felt bad for not telling Dylan and Malory about what she was doing, but she hoped they'd understand.

"We're counting on it," Dylan replied, smoothing out Morello's saddle pad.

Honey followed Lani away from the three Chestnut Hill vans and across the crowded field. They couldn't see the main school buildings from the paddocks, although when they'd come up the driveway, there had been signs at every fork. Allbrights was obviously a huge campus.

There were so many riders that the competition was being held outside in three roped-off rings surrounded by temporary seating. Even though the first class wasn't scheduled to start for an hour, some of the school teams were already warming up. A flashy palomino trotted past, followed by a dark bay gelding that had to be at least seventeen hands high. Their riders were wearing the aqua team colours of Wycliffe School.

"The competition looks pretty intense," Lani commented as they weaved their way to the gate at the far end of the field.

Honey nodded. Although she wasn't about to back

out on Plan B, she felt a twinge of disappointment that she wouldn't be able to cheer for the Chestnut Hill team today. She pulled out her mobile phone again to check for missed calls. Her screen was blank, so she shoved it back into her pocket. She had to face the facts: her mom wasn't going to call to say she was coming to bring her to the hospital. Maybe she hadn't checked her voice mail; maybe she wasn't prepared to go back on her previous decision. Honey was going to have to get there on her own.

She and Lani had noticed a bus stop that was about a ten-minute walk back along the main road. All Honey had to do was get there without being seen. They'd decided that if she was stopped, she should stick to the truth as much as possible and say she was going to visit her brother in the hospital.

Honey glanced nervously over her shoulder as they reached the gate. She felt like hundreds of eyes were following her.

"No one's watching," Lani reassured her. She gave Honey a quick hug. "Tell your brother that we're all rooting for him, OK?"

"I will," Honey promised. "Thanks a million for this, Lani."

"I'll see you later," Lani told her. "You can tell me exactly how much better Sam is feeling because he's seen you."

Honey felt a weight lift off her. She hoped with all her heart that her visit was going to make a difference to her brother. *Please don't let me be wrong about this.*

She slipped through the gate and down the road, past tennis courts, a baseball field, and a hockey field. Through a strip of shady beech trees, she caught a glimpse of the Allbrights school buildings. They were sleek and modern, with huge blue-tinted windows set into dark red brick. Honey preferred Chestnut Hill, with the Old House building that was over a hundred years old – ancient in American terms, even though her house in England had been built well before that.

The road widened into a tree-lined avenue. As a truck with a horse trailer drove through the main gates, Honey had to fight the urge to hide behind a tree. Instead she kept her head high and carried on like she had every reason to be heading out of the school gates. The vehicle rumbled past without stopping, and Honey forced herself not to look back, her heart pounding as loud as the truck engine.

Cheney Falls was still a few miles away, but she and Lani had checked out a bus timetable back at school. She knew that buses ran regularly past Allbrights. She needed the Q90, which stopped at the hospital about halfway along its route.

A rumbling grew steadily louder behind her. A bus drove past, and Honey broke into a run to reach the stop at the end of the lane. She was completely out of breath by the time she jumped on board the bus, but at least it meant she wouldn't have to hang around in the open until another bus pulled up.

She sat down alongside a woman wearing a thick coat, hat, scarf, and gloves, like she was expecting a blizzard. Honey suddenly realized that she hadn't checked the number of the bus before getting on. *What if I end up going to the wrong end of town?*

"Excuse me. What number bus is this?" she asked the woman beside her.

"The Q90," the woman told her.

Honey let out a sigh of relief and settled back in her seat. For the first time, she began to worry about what her parents would say when she turned up at the hospital. Honey lifted her chin stubbornly. Maybe it was time her parents learned that she could handle Sam's illness better than they thought.

Honey had been a little worried that she wouldn't recognize the hospital, but there was no mistaking the tall, glass-sided building that towered above one of the bus stops. White-coated medical staff were bustling through the sliding doors at the entrance, and several other passengers disembarked with her when the bus stopped. Honey took a deep breath as she walked across the parking lot and through the main doors. There was a map of the hospital on the wall in the foyer, and Honey quickly located the children's unit in oncology before taking a lift up to the fourth floor. There was a ping, and the doors opened onto the oncology ward, with the nurses' station just in front of her. *I made it!*

Honey walked up to the desk. "Hi, I'm here to see Sam Harper," she said nervously.

The dark-haired receptionist smiled. "May I have your name, please?"

"Felicity Harper," Honey replied, gripping her hands behind her back to keep them from shaking. Why couldn't they just take her to him?

"Is Sam expecting you?" the woman asked. Her tone was pleasant, but to Honey this felt like a police interrogation. Her heart began to beat faster, and her palms felt clammy.

"You have to let me see him. I've come especially." To her horror, she felt her throat tighten and a prickling at the back of her eyes. It couldn't be possible that Sam was only a couple of metres away and she might not be allowed to see him.

The receptionist lifted her phone. "I'll put a call through to his room and see if he is ready for visitors."

Honey stared at her, blinking her eyes to keep back the tears. What if Sam's doctor said no? Or worse still, what if Sam said he couldn't see anyone? He might not realize who had come to visit him! This was a stupid plan. She should have waited for her mom to tell her it was OK to come.

"Honey?"

Honey spun around. Her father was walking up the corridor, carrying two cups of coffee.

"Dad!" She raced toward him, the tears she'd been fighting to hold back spilling down her cheeks. He only just had time to put the coffee on a nearby chair before she flung herself into his arms. "I'm sorry, Dad, I had to come. And now they might not let me in! I've got to see him, Dad, please!"

Her father held her close. "It's OK, sweetheart.

Calm down." After a few moments, he wiped away her tears gently before murmuring in her ear, "I'll go sort things out, just give me a second."

Feeling very small and helpless, Honey watched as her dad walked over to the desk and said something to the receptionist. He called Honey over. "It's OK, you can come in."

Honey took a shuddering breath. It felt like her knees were about to give out on her. "Which way?"

"He's just through here," said her dad, leading her down the corridor to a private room. He hesitated with his hand on the door handle. "Sam looks a lot different from the way he was at Thanksgiving. He's wired up to a machine and drips."

"I know. We went through a bone-marrow transplant together, remember?" Honey said. But inside, her stomach was tying itself in knots. She'd been so caught up in the logistics of getting to the hospital that she hadn't imagined the moment when she'd actually get to see her twin. Was she ready for this? Would she be able to deal with it? Sam had always been the strong one.

Her dad pushed open the door. A high metal-frame bed stood in the middle of the room, surrounded by bleeping machines and complicated-looking equipment. Honey stopped dead in the doorway, her hand flying to her mouth to hide her gasp. She thought she'd seen Sam at his sickest, but nothing could have prepared her for this. She hardly recognized her brother. He'd lost pounds of weight. His arms looked blue against the sheets, and his eyes seemed deep in their sockets. His lips were dry and cracked. *Oh, Sam.* Even his thick blond hair had been shorn close to prepare for the chemo.

"Honey!" Her mother stood up from a chair drawn close to Sam's bed. "What are you doing here?"

Sam's eyes opened, and he shifted his head on the pillow so he could look at Honey. His lips tugged upward as his blue gaze focused on her. One thing never changed about her twin – the jewell brightness of his eyes. "I knew you'd come," he whispered.

Honey smiled back, her heart flooded with relief that she had done the right thing after all. "I knew you'd know."

Out of the corner of her eye, she saw her dad shake his head at her mom, warning her not jump in with a load of questions. There was an empty chair on the other side of the bed, and Honey sat down, grateful that her legs had gotten her this far. She reached for Sam's hand; his fingers felt brittle and cold. "How are you feeling?"

"You mean you don't know?" Sam teased weakly.

Honey solemnly pressed her finger against his forehead and then transferred it to her own. It was an old game they'd thought up years ago, when people were desperate to believe they had psychic twin powers and could read each other's minds.

"You've been trapped in a dark, dark place. But now a ray of light has appeared, and amazingly, your despair is lifting." She smiled.

"Something like that." Sam grinned. He gave her hand a faint squeeze. "I'm glad you came."

"Me, too," said Honey, but she shot an uneasy glance at her parents.

"Does anyone at school know where you are right now?" her mom asked worriedly.

Honey swallowed. There was no way she was going to mention Lani, in case her friend got into trouble for helping her. "Actually, no. I'm supposed to be at a horse show with Ms Carmichael." The inside of her mouth felt dry. Leaving school without permission was a major transgression. *Will I be expelled?*

"I'll phone Dr Starling," said Mr Harper. "She can call Ms Carmichael's mobile and tell her where Honey is." He stood up and held out his hand to Honey's mom. "Let's rescue the coffee I left outside and let the twins have some time together."

The twins. It was good to hear those words again.

Mrs Harper ran her hand through her shoulder-length blonde hair. Honey realized her mom looked exhausted and knew she hadn't helped by running away from school. She was about to apologize when her mom came over and gave her a hug. "Let Sam sleep when he gets tired."

"I will," Honey promised. She had a sudden urge to thank her mom and dad for letting her see Sam, but she wasn't sure how to start. She decided simply to smile at her mom as warmly as she could.

As soon as her parents were gone, she turned back to Sam. "OK, tell me how you really are."

"Not as bad as I was a couple of days ago," Sam admitted weakly. "I'd forgotten how much chemo knocks out of you."

"But you didn't react to it like this before." Honey frowned. "What's different this time?"

"Who knows?" Sam's eyelids were looking heavy. "I'm just glad you're here."

"Me, too." Honey felt her throat close with emotion. "I've missed you so much, Sam." The room was quiet, and Honey let her words sink in.

"You like it at Chestnut Hill, don't you?"

Honey nodded. "Yeah, it's great."

"It sounds like you've made some really good friends," Sam murmured, his eyes closing.

"Yeah. They're the best." Honey leaned back in her chair, without letting go of Sam's hand. The last few nights of broken sleep were catching up with her.

"Honey?"

"Yeah?" She'd thought he was asleep.

"I know what you're like. It doesn't hurt to talk, you know. When things get tough, it's good to have friends."

Honey had an uneasy feeling deep in her stomach. She didn't like where the conversation was heading.

"You can't depend on me for everything," Sam persisted.

"Don't talk like that," Honey begged him, squeezing his hand.

As Sam's breathing grew deeper and more even, Honey couldn't stop his words from replaying in her head louder and louder until she felt they would deafen her. I'll never let you go, she vowed. She looked down at his thin fingers, curled in her hand. *You got better once, you can do it again. I know you can.* Then she pressed her index finger to her forehead and transferred it to his. *I know you can.*

She leaned back in her chair again. She was here now. That was all that mattered.

Honey stirred as the door opened. She blinked, feeling disoriented for a moment before she remembered she was at the hospital. She didn't know how long she'd slept. She glanced to see her brother was still sleeping deeply. Honey gently disentangled her hand from his and turned in her chair.

Oh no! She jumped up, her heart pounding louder than a freight train.

Mrs Herson was standing in the doorway.

Chapter Twelve

Honey walked toward her housemother, feeling her cheeks burn. *I'd do this a hundred times over if it was the only way I could visit Sam.* She met Mrs Herson's eyes, wondering if she'd understand.

Mrs Herson didn't say anything as she stepped back into the corridor. Her face was totally unreadable. Honey caught sight of someone over her housemother's shoulder. She blinked. What was Lani doing here? *Mrs Herson must have found out that Lani helped me get here.* Honey felt terrible. The last thing she'd wanted was to land her best friend in trouble.

Lani met her eyes and mouthed, "Sorry." Before Honey could respond, her parents hurried toward them.

"Mrs Herson!" Honey's mother exclaimed. "We'd have driven Honey home. You didn't need to have come for her."

Mrs Herson smiled. "Please don't worry. After we got your call at school, I tried to get hold of Ms Carmichael but she didn't answer her cell phone. I thought it was best to drive over to Allbrights, to let her know what was happening, and then came here. How is Sam?"

"Not great." Mrs Harper's smile was strained, and Honey's dad slipped his arm around her.

They started to give Mrs Herson some details about Sam's condition, and Honey left them to talk to Lani.

"I'm really sorry," Lani burst out, keeping her voice low. "Hersie showed up at Allbrights and made it clear that she knew where you were. Ms Phillips told her that the last time she saw you was when we went to go get drinks, so Mrs Herson guessed I probably knew where you'd gone."

"*I'm* sorry," Honey said. "I'll tell Mrs Herson it was all my fault."

"Don't worry," said Lani. "I think Hersie was too worried about you to bawl me out. What did your parents say about you just turning up? They must have been totally freaked."

"I haven't had a chance to talk to them much," Honey admitted. "I chatted with Sam for a while, and then we both fell asleep."

Lani shook her head, smiling. "I come up with one of my amazing plans to get you here, and all you end up doing is taking a nap?"

"That's OK. Sam fell asleep first." Honey grinned. "Great bedside company I turned out to be!"

"His chemo must be really taking it out of him," Lani said seriously as Mrs Herson came over.

"Your parents would like to speak with you, Honey.

Lani and I will go get some coffee in the cafeteria."

Lani shot Honey a sympathetic glance as she got up and headed to the lift with their housemother.

Honey's parents came to sit down with her. They were quiet while a doctor walked up the corridor and went into Sam's room. Honey saw an anxious look flit between her parents. *Are they expecting bad news?*

"Is that Sam's doctor?"

"One of them," said her dad. "I expect he'll talk to us after he's seen Sam. Let's hope he's going to say your brother's responding to the treatment."

Honey nodded. She took a deep breath and got straight to the point. "I know you must be really angry with me for coming here."

"Actually we're pretty angry at ourselves. We didn't really give you a choice," Honey's dad replied. "We thought we were doing what was best for you and Sam, but we obviously didn't understand."

Whoa! Honey felt like she'd been torpedoed. She'd expected her parents to be upset with her for leaving the show ground and coming across town on her own, without letting one of the faculty members know where she was. They'd made it clear they wanted her to stay in school until they felt Sam was ready to see her.

"All we wanted to do was protect you both, you know that, don't you?" her mom said anxiously. "You're both so precious to us. We thought that it would be best to separate you so we could concentrate on nursing Sam while you had some sort of normality at school."

Honey met her mom's steady green gaze. "I do know that all you've ever wanted is the best for me, the best for both of us." She took a deep breath. "But keeping me apart from Sam isn't the best thing for either of us. The less I see him, the more I worry about him."

Her dad's mouth creased with pain. Honey noticed that his blue eyes were bloodshot with fatigue, and her heart tugged at how hard Sam's illness was hitting her whole family.

"Honey, I'm so sorry," said Mr Harper. "Your mother and I didn't want you to be affected by Sam's treatment the way you were when you lived at home. We phoned Mrs Herson regularly to keep her up-to-date and to check that you were OK. She seemed to think you were doing fine. But I guess you were just doing a good job of hiding the way you were really feeling. I'm sorry if we made you feel like that was what you had to do."

"Chestnut Hill is great," Honey said quickly. "I'm happy there, I promise. What was driving me crazy was the feeling you weren't being honest with me. I was with Sam when he had his last round of treatment. What made you think I wouldn't be able to cope this time? I don't see why I couldn't have come home on weekends to be with him. It felt like I was being shut out. Like I couldn't do anything for him – or for you."

Mrs Harper slipped her arm around Honey's shoulder. "That's the last thing we wanted you to feel. You always sounded like you were having a great time at school." She blinked and wiped a finger under her eyes. "I keep forgetting how strong you are."

"I'm not so strong when I can't be with Sam and you guys," Honey said, leaning her head against her mom's shoulder.

"And we need you, too," declared her mom. "From now on the Harpers stick together. Even though you're in school, it doesn't mean you can't come home any weekend you like. I'm sure Sam would be happier with that, too. I promise we won't ever again make decisions about you without talking to you first."

Honey held out her little finger and crooked it. It was something she and Sam had always done when they made a promise. Her dad smiled and linked his finger with hers, and her mom did the same.

"That's it, then," Honey said. "If you break the promise, your finger will fall off." She smiled, and her dad went to ruffle her hair.

"Oh, I forgot, you haven't been into me messing your hair since you were six," he said, snatching back his hand.

"You guys aren't the only ones to sometimes get things wrong," Honey said. "You can ruffle my hair anytime. Except," she added, ducking as her dad reached out again, "when we're out in public!"

Her dad chuckled and gave her a hug. "I'm not going to say that breaking out of school today was a good move, but it's wonderful to see you and be able to talk properly. It's something we've all been avoiding, I think."

You've got that right! Honey thought.

"Do you want to say goodbye to Sam before Mrs Herson drives you back?" her mom asked as the doctor came out of Sam's room.

Honey nodded, getting up from her seat.

"Oh, and, Honey," her mom called just before Honey opened Sam's door, "why don't you tell Sam you'll be back next weekend?"

Honey grinned. "It's a deal."

Sam was awake and propped up on his pillows. Honey thought he looked even paler than before – if that was possible. "One of the doctors just finished poking and prodding me," he explained in a voice that was barely louder than a whisper.

"I won't stay long," Honey said. "I just wanted to say goodbye."

Sam looked disappointed. "You're going already?"

"I've probably taken up way more visiting time than I'm allowed, even if I am your twin," Honey said, walking over to his bed. "My housemother just came to take me back to school. She figured Lani was in on the whole thing, too. That's how she found out I was here."

"I hope Lani doesn't get into trouble," Sam said faintly.

"Mrs Herson hasn't said anything yet, but I expect she's saving the lecture for the trip back," Honey admitted. "Lani didn't seem too upset about it, but then that's her style. She always comes across like she can handle anything."

"You talked to her?"

"She's here," Honey told him. "She came with Mrs Herson."

"Can you do me a favour and sneak her in?" Sam asked, his blue eyes brightening. "I'd like to meet her. And thank her for helping you with her strategy."

"Hey, I get some credit, you know." Honey pretended to be insulted.

"Yeah, but you're Honey," Sam said, straight-faced.

"You know, if you weren't in a hospital bed. . ." Honey shook her fist at her brother.

"You'd do your best to put me in one." He grinned. "Why do you think I'm getting in all of my insults now before I'm up and about again?"

Honey looked at Sam and smiled. *Up and about again.* That sounded good. "I'm going to hold you to that."

Sam swallowed and looked down at his hands. "Honey, tell me the truth. Did you think there was a chance that I wouldn't be?"

Honey tried to hide her expression, but there was no point. They may not have been telepathic, but Sam could always get right into her head. "Sometimes I get scared," she admitted. "I thought we had it beat once. When it came back. . ." Her voice trailed off as she remembered how angry and terrified she'd felt on Thanksgiving.

Sam lifted his chin and stared at her.

Honey pulled a loose thread from her shirt and began to twist it around her finger. "I don't know how you keep so positive," she said. "And then I don't feel I can say how I'm really feeling because you're so brave all the time."

Sam closed his eyes. "Maybe I'm not as brave as you think."

"You are," Honey protested. "You're always so upbeat about fighting this thing. And I want to be positive, too; but sometimes when I hear myself rambling on and on about stuff at school, I just want to tell myself to shut up. It all seems so trivial, compared with what you're going through."

Sam flinched, and his eyes flew open. "Don't ever start thinking that, Honey. It may seem trivial, but hearing about your friends and your life at school keeps me going when I'm really low. It helps to know that things are different for you." He shook his head against his pillow. "Listen, I want you to do something for me. I want you to pretend you're me. Pretend you're the one who's sick. Would you want me to sit around a hospital fossilizing or would you want me out there living my life?"

Honey's stomach twisted as she thought of all the times she'd longed to trade places with her twin. "No," she admitted. "I'd want you out there, living it up."

Sam let out a deep breath. "Sometimes I think it's harder on you, being the healthy one," he said slowly. "If you were the one who was sick, I'd want to change places with you instead of watching you go through all this, knowing there's nothing I can do to help."

"Sam." Honey choked on his name.

"But there isn't anything you can do. So promise me

you'll take advantage of being out there," Sam urged. "Then you can tell me all about it. I bet your friend Lani could show you a trick or two."

Honey bent down and hugged her brother as close as she could, navigating around all the wires and monitors. She couldn't put how she was feeling into words, but she was relieved to know she didn't have to try. Sam already understood. "I'll go see if Lani's around."

Lani and Mrs Herson were just getting out of the lift when Honey opened Sam's door. She waved Lani over. When Honey led her into the room, she suddenly wondered what her friend would think of the difference between the cute boy in the photo and how he was now, so pale he was practically transparent. Maybe Lani would feel uncomfortable – after all, Honey hadn't given her any warning about how sick Sam looked.

But Lani's expression didn't change when she saw Sam. "Hi, Sam," she said walking straight up to his bed. "How you doing?"

"Great, thanks," he smiled. "Ignore the machines. I'm just using this whole chemo thing to play truant. I was getting sick of biology."

"Hey, that's a good idea. Maybe that would work for my next history assignment. Honey *has* to have told you the teacher is a nightmare," Lani said, sitting down on a chair alongside the bed.

Something about this felt weird to Honey. She had struggled so long to get here and to be able to talk freely with Sam, and now Lani comes right in and sits down – with no long sighs and difficult words. But Honey guessed that was part of why they each reminded her of the other – Sam and Lani were both witty, and fast to make friends.

"Sorry, I've already patented it. Chemo is my get-out-of-school card. You'll have to come up with your own idea," Sam told her.

"This is a girl who can plot, plan, or plead her way around anything," Honey teased. "That won't be a problem."

"Yeah?" Sam lay back against his pillows. "We should exchange notes sometime." His eyelids flickered.

"Definitely," Lani said, looking over at Honey. She raised her eyebrows questioningly toward the door. She'd obviously noticed how tired Sam had gotten.

Honey nodded.

As Lani stood up and turned away from the bed, Honey noticed a look of worry shoot across her face. *Seeing Sam like this must be pretty tough for her. She's hiding it well.*

"It was great meeting you," Sam said drowsily.

"You, too." Lani's voice was warm. "I was already a fan of one half of the Harper twins. I guess now I'm rooting for the whole team." She smiled at Honey. "I'll wait outside, OK?"

Honey watched her leave the room. "Isn't she great?" she said as soon as the door closed.

"Yeah, she's just what I pictured. If the rest of your friends are like her, I can see why you like Chestnut

Hill so much," Sam agreed in a whisper. "Thanks for coming, Honey. It means a lot to me." He reached for her hand.

"Me, too," she said, leaning down to hug him one last time. "I don't want to go, but I better not push my luck with Mrs Herson." She straightened up. "I'll be back to see you next weekend. Mum said it will be OK for me to come." Honey just hoped Mrs Herson would let her off the grounds. There was a chance she would have her off-site privileges revoked.

"That's great." His voice sounded very far away. "If you don't come, maybe it will be my turn to break out of here to get to you."

"Nah, my friends have seen your photo, and for some reason they think you're totally hot. You'd have to beat them off with a stick if you turned up at school," Honey joked.

"Sounds like a lot of work." Sam's words slurred. Honey leaned down and kissed his cheek, then softly stepped away from the bed.

She stopped at the door to take one last look at her brother. *No matter what punishment Mrs Herson decides on, today has been worth it.*

Mrs Herson pulled up in the staff parking lot at the back of the Chestnut Hill stable block. She shut off the car's engine before turning in her seat to look at Honey and Lani. "I know I don't have to tell you how serious leaving school without permission is," she began.

Honey and Lani nodded. *Here we go*, Honey thought.

"And to leave when you were representing the school at an outside event was even worse. You were breaking rules that are there for your own safety. And not only that, you were also breaking our trust in you."

Honey's mouth felt dry. "It was all my fault."

"No, it wasn't," Lani said quickly. "It was my idea."

Mrs Herson held up her hand. "I don't want to know the details, because then I might have to start assigning detentions."

Honey swapped a startled look with Lani. "You mean you're not going to?"

"As far as I see it, you went to visit your brother, who is very sick in the hospital. For the most part, you were under your parents' supervision," Mrs Herson summarized. "I think that's all to be said about this afternoon's events. Besides, you both ended up missing the league competition, so I guess explaining that to your roommates will be punishment enough."

"Mrs Herson, I've always said you are the coolest housemother," Lani breathed.

"Save it for when I'm handing out detentions for messy rooms and breaking curfew," Mrs Herson said dryly. "And if you ever even think about going anywhere – even to the hospital – absent without official leave again, I won't go easy on the punishment. Honey. . ." she added as the girls got out of the car.

"Yes, Mrs Herson?"

"Don't forget I'm always here, if you need to talk."

She paused. "I really hope Sam is going to pull through."

Honey felt her throat tighten. "Thank you."

She followed Lani along the path that led to the barn. "You missed the competition, too?" she asked.

"I saw Eleanor and Olivia go clear, but then Hersie turned up," Lani explained.

"So we got two clear rounds?" Honey felt a burst of excitement. She couldn't wait to find out how the others had gone.

Inside the barn the horses were all blanketed and munching from their hay nets. The radio was turned up in the tack room; and through the open door, Honey could see the riding teams busily cleaning their saddles. She glanced at her watch. It was twenty past five. She'd been gone nearly a whole day.

"Hey, strangers. Now's the time to make an appearance, just when we've finished up," Dylan teased, threading a stirrup leather back onto Morello's saddle.

"Is everything OK? Ms Carmichael said that Mrs Herson picked you both up from the show." Malory looked at them with concern.

They think Mrs Herson took us both. They don't know I left on my own. So they don't know where I've been. Honey's mind whirled. The last thing she wanted to do was announce the truth to all the competition riders. The truth was hard enough to share with friends.

"Hersie needed our help," Lani said quickly.

Dylan frowned. "What help did she need that took you away from the show?"

Honey stared helplessly at Lani.

"She needed to collect some food supplies for our Christmas party tomorrow," Lani said. "It was only supposed to be a quick ten-minute job. Get us, park outside the store in town to load up, bring us back to the show."

"And?" prompted Eleanor Dixon when Lani stopped, expecting a grand excuse for their missing the event.

"Her car broke down." Lani sounded casual as she stooped to pick up a sponge that Malory had dropped. "It took hours before it was fixed. Can you believe it?"

"No," Dylan said, narrowing her eyes. "I can't."

Change the subject – quick! "So I take it we didn't win a ribbon?" Honey ventured.

"Can't have," Lani agreed. "It's the reason they're giving us such a hard time."

"Well, maybe if we'd had you two cheering us on, the red ribbon would have been within reach," said Olivia Buckley.

"As it is we had to settle for a blue," Dylan sighed.

"No way!" Honey exclaimed. The team had placed second in their first major All Schools League event! She looked at Malory. "So Tybalt did OK?"

"Apart from knocking the stile, he was amazing." Malory's eyes lit up. "He jumped everything else as if he had wings. He didn't even freak out when he was pinned against the rail by this giant bay during the practice session. He's really mellowing out."

"We've decided to stage a protest if Tybalt isn't

allowed to stay," Dylan said. "Even Lynsey said she'd wave a banner."

Lynsey rolled her eyes as she took her saddle over to the rack on the wall. "I would hardly wave a banner. It's just that Tybalt obviously has good breeding that decided to make an appearance today. I still think he's unpredictable."

"Team spirit, please," Eleanor interrupted. "At least until we finish cleaning our tack."

"Well, we're not going to finish anytime soon at this rate," Lynsey replied, squeezing past Olivia to reach her seat and draping her bridle across her knees. "There's not enough room to think in here."

"I think that's our cue to leave," Lani said to Honey.

"No, it's your cue to empty this." Dylan grinned, holding out her bucket of dirty, soapy water.

"No worries," Lani said. "Do you want more clean water?"

Dylan nodded. "Please."

"I think I might go check on Minnie," Honey said to Lani as they left the tack room. She hesitated. "Thanks again for today, and covering for me back there."

"That's what friends are for," Lani told her cheerfully. She held up the bucket of dirty water. "That and providing manual labor! Good thing I've got broad shoulders so they're willing to keep me around."

Honey laughed as Lani carried the bucket out to the tap. She walked down to Minnie's stable, anticipating the grey mare's friendly whicker. It didn't come, and she stared in dismay at the empty stable. *She's not here!*

Could her legs have become much worse in one day? Then Honey remembered Kelly saying she was going to turn her out in the paddock that afternoon.

She jogged out of the barn and down the path that led to the turnout paddocks. Kelly was leading Minnie toward her. Honey studied the way she was walking and was thrilled when she couldn't spot any sign of lameness. The grey mare pricked her ears as soon as she saw Honey and let out a loud whinny.

"How did she go?" Honey asked, out of breath, as she rubbed Minnie between the eyes.

"She really enjoyed herself," Kelly replied enthusiastically. "I went to bring her in half an hour ago, but she and Nutmeg were busy grooming each other. I couldn't bear to break them up."

Honey pictured Minnie and the cute buckskin, nibbling the base of each other's manes. "I wish I'd seen that. But there'll be plenty of other times, I know."

Kelly glanced over to Honey and clicked to Minnie to walk on. "I know you've got a great bond with Minuet," she began.

"I know she's not mine," Honey jumped in. She guessed Kelly, like Ms Carmichael, was trying to find a way to warn her not to get too involved. Now that Minnie was recovering, Patience would be the one riding her and spending time with her. "But I can still enjoy her company. Patience can't ban me from standing outside her stall and giving a carrot or two!"

Kelly didn't reply. Puzzled, Honey shot her a look and noticed the stable hand anxiously biting her lip.

"Look, it's not for me to say anything, but I think you should be prepared."

Prepared for what? She was starting to worry Honey.

"Mr Duvall's disappointed that Patience hasn't been completely dedicated to looking after Minuet," Kelly admitted. "He feels Minnie deserves a home where she's more appreciated, not treated like a plaything that can be picked up or put down whenever her owner feels like it."

Honey stared at Kelly in dismay. "He's thinking of selling her?" No other pony had come close to the way she'd felt about Rocky until now. *This can't be happening.*

"I shouldn't have said anything. It's just that I know how much you've put into caring for her," Kelly said, shortening her hold on the rope as she prepared to lead Minnie into the barn. "It's a shame, really. If Patience had acted more like you, none of this would be an issue."

Honey dropped back as Kelly led the mare through the barn's double doors. She wrapped her arms around herself, feeling as if she'd just been hit with a heavy weight. *Minnie can't leave Chestnut Hill. She just can't!*

Chapter Thirteen

Honey raced down to the barn early the next morning. If Minnie was going to be sold, she wanted to spend as much time with her as possible. She had to take time out later in the day to prepare for the Adams Christmas party, but she was determined to spend the morning in the barn. *At least I don't have to worry about an outfit*, Honey thought, glad that it was a pyjama party they'd arranged. Not all of the girls were taking the dress-down theme seriously, though. Lynsey and Patience had actually booked into a salon to have their hair and nails done, so Honey knew she wouldn't have to worry about running into them at the barn!

Honey opened the main barn door. Inside it was warm and hay-scented, compared to the crisp, chilly air outside. None of the horses were looking over their doors. Honey peered over the nearest partition and saw Foxy Lady with her head thrust into her feed bowl. "Morning," she murmured before hurrying down to Minnie's stall.

Kelly was running a brush over Minnie's neck. "I was

hoping you would turn up," she said, smiling over her shoulder at Honey. "I'm taking Minuet out for some exercise before she has her breakfast. I don't suppose you'd like to help out?"

"Try stopping me," Honey replied as Minnie swung her head around to blow a welcome through her nostrils.

Kelly buckled Minnie's lunging cavesson before leading her out of her stall. *She's still a bit stiff,* Honey thought, standing back to watch the mare's action. But that was probably because she'd been standing in the stable overnight; she'd loosen up once she'd had a chance to stretch her legs in the arena.

Kelly halted Minnie in the centre of the ring. "Would you mind leading her for the first couple of circuits? She might be feeling full of energy after her week of box rest, and I don't want her rushing off. Just keep her steady until she works out that all I'm asking for is a gentle walk."

"I get it," said Honey, resting her hand on Minnie's cavesson to steer her to the outside of the arena. The mare stretched her nose out to sniff the air and snorted, shaking her mane.

"Does that smell good?" Honey smiled. Minnie let out a piercing neigh that was answered faintly from the turnout paddocks. "Don't worry, your friends are still there," Honey reassured her. "And I'm not going anywhere for a while."

"She's moving more freely than I thought, so let's give her a few strides at trot," Kelly called.

Honey nodded and tilted her head toward the pony. "Are you ready? Trot on, then, that's a good girl."

At first Minnie seemed reluctant to go any faster. Honey let go of the rein and ran a little way ahead. "Trust me, Minnie. Come on, follow me." She gave a few insistent clicks.

Keeping her dark eyes firmly fixed on Honey, Minnie broke into a slow trot.

"Good girl; that's brilliant," Honey praised.

Minnie was as obedient as any well-trained pony, but Honey sensed that she wasn't another Bluegrass. *It's not that she's been taught to obey commands; it's that she genuinely wants to. She likes being part of a team*, Honey realized. *She's a horse in a million, and Patience doesn't know what she's missing out on.* Honey's throat tightened. She couldn't believe she'd helped nurse Minnie back to health only for the sweet mare to be sold.

"I think that's enough for today," Kelly said after they'd completed another circuit. "I don't want to push her too much."

Honey nodded. "Do you want me to take her back to the barn?"

"Sure," said Kelly. "The way you two are together, I feel like I'm butting in on a private conversation anyway. She really gets you."

Honey took the rope, surprised to hear that Kelly thought they had a special bond. Honey had always believed that Minnie was that open with everyone. "Come on, Min, let's get you back to your nice, warm stable." Minnie swung her head around to nibble at Honey's jacket. Honey tangled her hand in the mare's thick mane, thinking about how Rocky had helped her through Sam's illness the first time around. This time, it seemed to be Minnie. Rocky had been both her escape and her friend. With Minnie it had been different. The grey mare had given Honey the chance to channel her attention into helping her get better. Honey swallowed the lump in her throat. *I've already had to say goodbye to Rocky. I don't want to have to say goodbye to you, too.*

Honey pulled on her favourite Campbell tartan pyjamas. She'd bought them on a trip to Edinburgh, Scotland, last Autumn when things were going well. She loved the soft, warm material.

"Those pyjamas are my favourite," Dylan said, slipping her feet into a pair of slippers.

Honey smiled as she unhooked her dark blue robe from the back of the closet door, remembering how her mom had tried to persuade Sam to buy a kilt. Her twin had refused point-blank, saying that the only time he was flashing his legs was on a rugby field – and if his mom thought he would ever wear a skirt, then she had another think coming!

Honey peered into the mirror on the wall, so she could tie her hair back. She was looking forward to telling Sam all about tonight.

"Do you think one of us should remind Lynsey this is a dress-down party?" Dylan asked, jerking her head at the bathroom door. "She must have been in there for like two hours."

"Lynsey doesn't do dress-down," Honey pointed out as she rapped on the door. "Are you ready yet?"

"No, go without me. I'll follow you down," Lynsey called back.

"This is going to be so great," Dylan said, spinning around to grab her terry cloth housecoat from her bed.

Honey nodded. If it wasn't for what she'd found out about Minnie, she'd be looking forward to the party a lot more.

"OK." Dylan's cheeks were already flushed with excitement as she looked at Honey. "All set?"

Honey quickly slid a lip-gloss wand over her bottom lip as her one concession to the fact that it was a party and not a sleepover. "Yup! Lead on!"

Christmas music filled the corridor from the open doorway of the senior lounge. Honey loved the silver-and-gold theme the seniors had chosen for the room. Sparkling icicle lights hung from the ceiling, and a huge Christmas tree stood in the far window recess, filling the air with the sweet smell of pine. Honey scanned the room, looking for Malory and Lani, but couldn't pick them out from all the girls dressed in pyjamas and robes.

"Hi!" Noel Cousins greeted Dylan and Honey with a warm smile.

"This is so great," Dylan enthused.

"Definitely the best dorm party on campus," Noel

agreed. "Christmas should be all about being relaxed and cosy!" Honey grinned when she noticed the cute slippers with pink bunny heads that Noel wore, the long ears reaching above her ankles. "The food's over there, whenever you're hungry," Noel said, pointing over to the kitchenette. A table covered with a gold cloth was laid out with a cold buffet.

"Hey, Noel, if this is supposed to be a party, where's the dancing?" Tanisha Appleton interrupted, her hands on her hips. "Merry Christmas, guys!"

"We cleared a space." Noel nodded to the middle of the room. "We just need some brave soul to kick things off. So are you volunteering?"

Tanisha looked thrown for a moment. She shrugged. "Sure. I can't dance on my own, though." She took hold of Noel's arm and dragged her over to the dance space, with Noel protesting between gasps of laughter.

Honey grinned at Noel's "rescue me" expression as Tanisha began twisting energetically to the music. Tanisha's silk ballerina slippers looked a lot easier to keep a beat in than Noel's pair of plush bunnies!

Dylan nudged her. "Am I seeing things?"

"Huh?" Honey followed Dylan's gaze to the buffet table. Someone was wearing bright red Santa pajamas, with a pillow stuffed inside the front and held in place with a black belt. Had one of the Saint Kits boys crashed their party?

Honey looked more closely. The person turned around, and she snorted with laughter. "Lani!"

Lani even had a fake snow-white beard and red cap.

192

As she headed toward them, she patted her stomach and let out a deep laugh. "Ho, ho, ho. Merry Christmas!"

"There's always one." Dylan grinned. "Can't we leave the crass commercialism of the holiday behind for one night?"

"That's not what it's about at all," Lani shot back. "My outfit says independent, witty, creative, individualistic."

"Just what every guy we know is looking for." Dylan grinned.

"What is every guy looking for?" Malory asked, joining them.

"A lumpy Santa." Dylan snorted with laughter, prodding Lani's padded stomach.

"That food looks amazing," Honey said, eyeing Malory's plate. "The food committee pulled out all the stops, by the look of it. I think we should go get some before it all disappears." She tugged Dylan over to the buffet table. Pumpkin pies, a chocolate Yule log, Santa biscuits, and a huge silver bowl full of frothy eggnog were laid out, along with spiced nuts, crackers, baked Brie, quiche, and salad.

"Hey, guys, did you remember to pin your baby photos on the board?" Malory asked as she ladled herself a cup of eggnog.

Lani nodded. "Lynsey collected them earlier and took charge of putting them up."

Honey couldn't help but remember that the Guess-the-Baby competition had led to Honey's friends learning about Sam. If Honey hadn't had to dig out a photo of herself as a baby, Dylan would never have pounced on his baby photo, and her friends would still be in the dark. Honey felt a stab of guilt. They knew about Sam, but only Lani knew the full truth. *Why am I still holding back?*

"Who's up for some Christmas carols?" Noel called.

There was a cheer as Faith, a senior who was applying for a music scholarship to Julliard, sat down at the electric piano and struck up "Jingle Bells."

"We're going for our turn at Guess-the-Baby," Lani whispered in Honey's ear. She picked up a handful of crisps. "Do you want to come?"

"Sure."

Lynsey was chewing on the end of a pen as she concentrated on the rows of baby photos. She was the only girl there who had opted for glamour over comfort, with a full-length satin nightgown. The silver material caught the hundreds of tiny lights on the ceiling with every movement Lynsey made. She'd even had tiny sparkling stones glued onto her nails. *She must have been hours at that salon.*

The girls picked up pen and paper from the table underneath the corkboard and stared at the photos. Honey frowned. This wasn't going to be easy!

"Oh, look at the bear." Razina and Wei Lin bent over the beautiful honey-coloured bear Mrs Herson had donated for the winner of the Guess-the-Baby contest. Someone had propped him up on the table beside the carton of pens.

"He's so cute!" Razina said, stroking the soft fur.

"Where have you been?" Lynsey demanded as

Patience joined them. "I thought you were going to put your hair up?"

"I didn't have time," said Patience, her cheeks looking flushed.

"You're already twenty minutes late," Lynsey said sharply. "What have you been doing?"

"I had to take a call from my dad." Patience pushed at a strand of hair that had fallen over her forehead. "I'll tell you about it later."

"Oh, right." Lynsey nodded like an unspoken message had passed between them. She turned her attention back to the baby photos.

Honey's stomach flipped over. *What if Mr Duvall called to say he's made up his mind to sell Minnie?*

"I'm just going to grab a drink," Patience said, flapping her hand in front of her face. "I'm really hot."

Honey left the others trying to match up the baby photos and followed Patience to the drinks table. She'd never be able to concentrate on the toddler snapshots unless she found out if there was any news about Minnie. "Um, Patience?"

"What?" Patience pulled back the tab on a can of soda.

Suddenly Honey didn't know what to say. *What did your dad want to talk to you about?* was hardly going to get Patience to open up. She'd tell Honey exactly what to do with her curiosity.

"It's starting to feel like I can't shake you," Patience said without smiling.

Yikes. Honey knew that the only thing she could do

was just jump straight in. "Was your dad calling about Minnie?"

"You're sounding obsessive about my pony again." Patience rolled her eyes. "You do know she's mine, don't you?"

"I heard that maybe she's not going to be here for much longer," Honey blurted out. *Oh, very subtle!* But she knew there was no going back now.

Patience narrowed her eyes. "How did you hear that? Sneaking around, listening in on my private conversations? I wouldn't put it past you, knowing you're friends with Dylan."

Honey didn't correct her, because she didn't want to get Kelly into trouble. "So is that what your dad wanted? To tell you that he's getting rid of Minnie?"

"You're being very dramatic about this," Patience sighed.

Honey's throat tightened. "Don't you care what happens to her?"

Patience looked at her in surprise. "Why would I want to ride a horse that has weak tendons? I need a horse that's going to be completely reliable in competition."

Honey tried to get a handle on her anger. If Patience had shown a bit more care toward Minnie in the first place, she wouldn't have strained her tendons; and none of this would be happening. "I'm sure Ms Carmichael will find her a good home," she said miserably.

"Duh!" Patience made a face. "Since she's keeping

Minuet for the riding school, then I think that goes without saying."

Honey stared at her. "Minnie's staying here?"

"I wanted Lynsey to be the first to know, so don't go blabbing it around," Patience warned. "That's what Dad called to tell me; that he's accepted Ms Carmichael's offer to keep Minnie here at no cost, to use for all the students."

Honey couldn't believe it! She suddenly felt a rush of happiness – not a run-around-the-room-screaming joy, but a very quiet, sweet one. Minnie was staying!

"Did you hear what I said?" Patience interrupted her thoughts.

Honey blinked. "Huh? Oh, yeah. I won't mention it to anyone. So this means she's going to be used as a riding-school horse?"

Patience rolled her eyes. "I might have guessed you'd want to get your mitts on her. All you've done since she arrived is try to take her over."

Unbelievable! Honey stared at Patience in disbelief. *If she'd taken care of Minnie, I wouldn't have got involved. So much for gratitude!* But then again Honey knew that she had been drawn to Minnie from the start; and she had been almost grateful that Patience wasn't interested in treating Minnie's injury.

"Just don't think it's forever," Patience warned. "Dad's only loaning her to Ms Carmichael on a monthly basis. I can have her back whenever I want." She glared at Honey for a moment before heading back to Lynsey.

What you mean is, you can have her back when you're ready to look after her properly, Honey thought shrewdly. Mr Duvall had really taken to his daughter's gorgeous pony, even if Patience herself hadn't. He'd made it clear all along that he wanted Minnie to have the best care – and he seemed well aware that Patience lacked the necessary dedication. There didn't seem to be much danger of that changing in the near future, which meant Honey would be able to spend as much time with Minnie as she could!

Honey hugged herself tight. She wanted to race down to the barn and throw her arms around the beautiful grey mare. She glanced down at her pyjamas. They weren't designed for wearing out on a cold December night. *Besides, I've pulled enough disappearing acts for one term.*

Honey felt her mobile phone vibrate in the pocket of her robe. No name popped up on the caller display, so Honey guessed it was her mom calling from the hospital.

Honey hurried out of the room. "Hello?" she said breathlessly. *Please, don't let it be bad news about Sam.*

"Whoa, why do you sound so desperate? I'm the one in the hospital." It was Sam.

"Sam! Since when do they have phones in intensive care?"

"I got early parole for good behavior." She could tell Sam was grinning.

"You're not in intensive care anymore?" Honey gripped the phone.

"They moved me to a regular ward. They're talking about me being home for Christmas, so you can forget any plans for a nice quiet holiday with Mum and Dad," Sam said. "I know you thought you'd get more presents and attention, but sorry. Hey, I called during your party, didn't I?"

"Don't worry," Honey told him. "What's important is that you're coming home! That is something worth celebrating." She thought back to when Sam had come home after the bone-marrow transplant. They'd all been convinced he had recovered that time as well. *I have to keep positive and believe that this time Sam will get better for good.*

"It was so great meeting Lani! Maybe I can get to meet the rest of your friends," Sam said. "They could come over for some of the Christmas break. Didn't you say Malory lives close by?"

"Yeah." Honey nodded. But Sam's words had sent her into a tailspin. The moment her friends saw her twin they would know he was very, very, sick. It would be obvious that Dylan had been right all along, and she'd been keeping even more secrets from them.

"Are you still there?" Sam asked.

"Yes, still here," Honey said quickly.

"You know, I was worried about you, having to deal with. . . with everything on your own. But I got it wrong. Lani and the rest of your friends are obviously helping you every step of the way."

Honey felt a spasm of guilt that Dylan and Malory were still shut out of the most important part of her life. She had to do something to fix that. Maybe it was best to tell them the truth now. If Sam was right, and he was getting better, it might be easier to share the news with them – without the fear of not knowing what could happen next. Honey had been worried that they would feel sorry for her and treat her differently. She still didn't want that, but she did want them to understand.

"Listen, I'll see you next weekend. Mum and Dad are picking me up on Saturday. And the weekend after that, I'll see you at home!"

"It's a deal," Sam said. "Have a great time at the party and take lots of photos, OK?"

"Ok," Honey promised before they hung up.

She walked back to the senior lounge as if her feet weren't quite touching the ground. It was such good news about Sam, she wasn't sure she could trust it, but she was going to try. She couldn't ask for anything more to make her happiness complete tonight, except for one thing. She knew there was something she had to do.

She found Malory and Dylan posing for pictures next to the Christmas tree. Malory was trying to fix Dylan's party hat, which kept slipping over one eye.

"Hey, you're just in time." Lani brandished her digital camera. "Go stand in the middle."

Honey linked arms with her friends but found it hard to smile. *Mal and Dylan think we're so close. They think we share everything with one another. It's like I'm lying to them every day. I feel like a fake.*

"Are you OK?" Mal asked. "Or are you wondering how we're going to handle being apart for Christmas break? Thanksgiving was hard enough!"

"Say Christmas cheese," Lani called, saving Honey from giving an answer.

"Sheesh, Honey, your family must need its own network with the amount of calls they make!" Dylan said once the camera flash had gone off. "Is everything OK?"

Honey met Lani's eyes, knowing she had to give her friends an honest answer. Lani nodded, as if she understood what Honey was thinking.

Honey knew her friends were there not just for what they could get out of their friendship, but also for what they could put in. *It's time to admit that I need them. After all, I don't know what's waiting for me around the next corner.*

Honey took a deep breath. "Let's go sit somewhere out of all the noise." She met Dylan's curious gaze and reached out for her hand. "There's something I need to tell you."

Have you read

Lauren Brooke's best-selling
Heartland series?

Heartland™

Amy's Journal

An extract...

"Nine hundred! Do I hear nine hundred?" the auctioneer's voice rang out above the noise of the crowd gathered in the sales barn. Standing around a circular pen, the onlookers watched as a pretty grey filly cantered around the pen, her head high.

A young woman standing near to me and Mom held up a card with a number on.

"That's nine hundred dollars to the lady in the green coat," the auctioneer said, nodding at the woman. "Do I hear any more?"

I looked at the grey filly. Her large dark eyes were fearful, her muscles were tense. I didn't like horse sales. The horses always looked so bewildered. I tried to imagine what it must be like for them, cantering around the noisy pen, not knowing why they were there or what was happening or who all these people were.

"Any more bids, ladies and gentlemen?" the auctioneer called. There was no response. He paused and then raised his hammer. "Going, going, gone!"

I glanced at the lady. She was smiling. I hoped that she would give the filly a good home.

"Next we have Lot 122," the auctioneer called as the pen gate was opened and the filly allowed out. An old bay hunter was next in the ring. He was skinny with a sway back, but he had a noble face and wise eye. He looked round in confusion and I felt awful. He looked like he should be grazing happily in a quiet field, and now who knew what would happen to him? A lot of the horses who came to a sale would end up being sold for meat. At the thought of the fate awaiting the bay in the ring, I felt suddenly sick.

"I need to get some fresh air," I said to Mom.

She nodded. "OK, I'll meet you by the trailer in half an hour."

I pushed my way through the crowd. The barn smelled of stale sweat and horse droppings. Reaching the entrance I walked outside and breathed in deep gulps of the damp March air. It was a relief to be outside, away from the scared horses and the shouting. Mom had come to the sales to see if there were any horses who needed Heartland's help. I just wanted to take them all home.

I looked around. Nearby was a barn with a cluster of metal pens. Each pen had a pony inside, waiting for their turn in the ring. The ponies were to be sold after the horses. Prospective buyers were now walking round the concrete walkways, examining the ponies and reading the notes attached to the pen gates.

I walked over. A brown-and-white paint pony was looking over the gate of the first pen. I stroked her nose and read her notes:

Lot 244: Scout. 13.2 h.h. mare. 15 years old. Has competed in equitation and hunter pony classes. 100% to load, shoe, clip and in traffic. Ideal first pony.

Scout nuzzled my hands and I fed her a horse-cookie from my pocket.

"She'd make you a lovely pony," a man standing nearby came over. "Are you looking to buy?"

"No. . . No, I'm not," I said, and hurriedly moved on.

There were so many ponies to look at. Old and young, all different shapes and sizes from a tiny black Shetland to a handsome bay hunter pony, whose card said it had won a string of prizes in the show-ring. As I walked towards the back of the barn, I saw a group of three men standing around a pen, their arms crossed.

"Unwarranted," I heard one of the men say, shaking his head.

I went closer. I couldn't see which pony they were discussing.

"Pity. He's a good-looking animal," the third man said, going closer to the pen gate. "And young too. Feed him up and you could get a good price for him."

There was a clatter of hooves. I saw a glimpse of a golden coat and heard a clang of metal as the pony threw himself at the pen gate. All three men jumped back.

"Vicious brute!" the first man shouted, waving his arms angrily. "Go on! Get back with you!"

The pony shot to the back of his pen. Shaking their heads, the men moved away and I saw the pony for the first time

He was beautiful, a buckskin with a dirty gold coat and a tangled black mane and tail. His head was high. His ribs stuck out and there were deep grooves in his quarters, but the look in his eyes was so full of pride and spirit that it seemed to make him glow with energy. He looked around, daring the world to come near him.

My eyes went to the card on his door. There was no name. Just the words:

Lot 247: 14.2 h.h. Gelding. 9 years old. Sold unwarranted.

• • •

I looked at the pony again. I felt drawn to him, to his fire, to his spirit.

"I wouldn't go too close to that pony, honey," a voice said behind me.

I swung round. One of the men who'd been by the buckskin's pen had seen me standing there and had come back.

"He's vicious," he told me. "He just tried to take a bite out of my friend." He shook his head. "The glue factory's the only place for a creature like him. You stay away from him or you'll get hurt." He nodded, walking off.

I hesitated and then looked back at the buckskin. He had tried to attack the men — I'd seen it. But was he really vicious? He looked so beautiful.

I scanned his face. His eyes were large and set high on his face. *Intelligent eyes. Proud eyes.* The words sprang into my mind and suddenly I remembered everything Mom had been teaching me about reading horses' faces. I could hear her voice in my head: "If a horse is behaving badly then look at his face. Do his features tell you he's mean and aggressive? If not then look for another reason for his behaviour — he may be in pain, he may be scared, he may simply be misunderstood."

I started to look more closely at the shape of the buckskin's features. His wide forehead signalled intelligence. His long narrow ears suggested he might be temperamental. He had large, defined nostrils — another sign of intelligence. And just above his nostrils, he had a bump. That, combined with his high-set proud eyes suggested he was a dominant horse who needed to be treated with respect. Everything about this nameless pony suggested he was intelligent and proud. He was stubborn, but not mean – certainly not vicious.

Just then a beam of sunlight flashed through a broken slat in the barn roof and danced on the pony's golden coat. His eyes flickered to mine. Suddenly I felt a charge rush through me, and I knew that I just had to persuade Mom to buy him.

"I'll be back," I told him and, turning, I ran down the aisle.

Mom was still beside the noisy ring. "Hi," she said, looking round as I pushed my way to her side. I was out of breath and she frowned. "What's up?"

"There's a pony!" the words burst out of me. "We've got to buy him, Mom! We've just got to!"

Mom looked surprised.

"Come and see him!" I begged. "Please!"

For a moment, Mom's eyes scanned mine and then to my relief, she nodded. "OK."

I turned and began to push my way out through the crowd. "Come on!"

Mom followed me.

As we got out of the auction barn, I started to tell her about the pony. "He's 14.2 hands, a buckskin. He's being sold as unwarranted. And has a vicious reputation, and likely that he'll go for meat. But he's not mean – not deep down. I know he's not."

"You read his face?" Mom said. It was half a question, half a statement.

I nodded. "You wait till you see him," I said, heading down the aisle that led to his pen. "You'll see what I mean."

The buckskin was still at the back of the barn, standing in his pen, his head raised.

I watched Mom's face as she scanned his head.

"Potentially stubborn," she said softly. "But very bright. Proud, brave, confident, complex – a pony who needs respect."

"That's what I thought!" I said in excitement. "It's his eyes and that bump on his nose."

The pony looked at us.

Mom read the card beside him. "So you heard some people say he's vicious?"

"I saw him try and bite them," I admitted.

"Why?" Mom asked curiously.

"One of the bidders went up to the gate," I replied. I looked at her beseechingly. "Can we buy him?"

"I'm not sure yet." Her eyes fixed on the pony, Mom stepped towards the gate. The pony's ears went back. Mom stopped and turned sideways on to him. She lowered her eyes. I knew what she was doing. By turning away from him and avoiding direct eye contact, she was trying to make herself seem as unaggressive as possible. By not walking up to the gate, she was respecting his space and waiting for him to make the first move. The minutes passed. Several people came by the pen, but when they saw that the card read "unwarranted" they walked away again. It was quiet near the back of the barn and no one took any notice of what Mom was doing – no one that is, apart from the pony. He watched her intently.

The first of the ponies to be auctioned was led out of the barn by a handler. Still Mom waited. Suddenly the buckskin snorted and brought his head down slightly. Mom took a small step away from him. He lowered his head even more and stared at her.

"That's it," she whispered. "Good pony."

He took a step towards her. There was nothing fearful about him, although his eyes showed a wariness. Step by step he moved closer to the gate until he was close enough to put his head over. He snorted again and then reached out with his muzzle and touched her shoulder.

Mom stayed very still for a moment, and then raised her hand and stroked his nose.

"There," she whispered. "You're not bad, are you?"

Slowly she backed away. The pony watched her and in his eyes, I saw a glimmer of softness.

Mom looked at me. "Yes," she said. "We can bid for him. He may have his problems, but deep down I think we'll find a very good pony in there."

I was delighted. "Oh, Mom, that's great! You really think we can help him?"

"No, but I think *you* can," Mom said.

I looked at her, wondering what she meant.

"You found him, Amy," Mom went on "You saw something in him that made you look beyond his behaviour. If we buy him then you should be the one to work with him."

"Me?" I stammered. I'd helped Mom with the horses, but I'd never worked with one on my own before.

Mom nodded. "You're more than ready to work with a horse on your own now, and I think this pony could be a very good starting point. I'll help you of course, but he'll be your responsibility. You can plan out his care, his training, you can work with him each day – if you want to."

I looked at the beautiful buckskin in delight. It would be like having a pony of my own. "Want to?" I exclaimed. "I'd love to!"

"Good," Mom smiled. "We'd better get ready to start bidding then."

"And now on to Lot 247," the auctioneer called. "A nine-year-old buckskin gelding. Sold unwarranted." There was the sound of shouting and the metal gate of the round pen swung open. The next instant the buckskin cantered into the ring, urged on by two handlers. Seeing the people, the pony stopped dead and pinned his ears back.

One of the handlers headed towards him. "Go on!" the man growled, swinging a rope.

The buckskin stared at him proudly and then, snaking his head down, he charged at the handler. With a yell, the man vaulted over the gate. Stopping with a defiant squeal, the buckskin stamped a front hoof down, sending a spray of sand into the air. A murmur of surprise ran through the crowd

The auctioneer cleared his throat. "So, Lot 247," the auctioneer said. "As you can see, a spirited pony. . ."

"Vicious, more like!" someone called from the crowd.

The auctioneer ignored the call. "What am I bid?"

I looked round anxiously. If the price went too high we wouldn't be able to buy the pony and right at that moment I wanted him more than anything else in the world.

The pony shook his head and squealed again.

"Who will start the bidding at six hundred dollars," the auctioneer asked.

No one in the crowd moved. Pinning back his ears the buckskin charged at the front row of people. They drew back hurriedly as he thudded into the barrier.

"Five hundred?" the auctioneer said. "Four hundred and fifty."

His voice was sounding increasingly desperate.

I glanced at the little group of meat-men. For once even their hands were still. The pony was skinny and trouble.

"Come on, ladies and gentlemen," the auctioneer encouraged. "A nice-looking pony like this. What am I bid?"

"One hundred and fifty dollars," Mom said, her voice ringing out

There was a surprised murmur. Everyone turned to look in our direction.

"One hundred and fifty dollars!" the auctioneer exclaimed. "Any advance on one hundred and fifty dollars? Look at his head, ladies and gentlemen, there's breeding in that head – he'd make a nice little pony, just needs some work. You're not seriously expecting me to sell a pony like this for one hundred and fifty."

The pony charged again at the fence and the audience gasped.

Seeming to decide that enough was enough, the auctioneer hastily brought his hammer up. "Going to the lady in the blue jacket on my left. Going, going, gone," he said, the words rushing out of him as he banged the hammer down to close the sale. The clerk wrote down Mom's number and I hugged Mom in delight. The pony was mine!

It took four handlers to get the pony out of the ring and back into his pen. Mom went to the office and paid and we fetched a halter from the trailer. "I want you to try and get the halter on to him," Mom said as we walked to the pen. "Just do what I did before. Stand and wait for him to make the first move."

"When do I put the halter on?" I asked.

"When you feel he's ready," Mom said.

The pony was standing at the back of the pen, his body tense. We stopped a couple of metres away from his gate. He stared at us and then snorted. It was as though he recognized us.

I walked forward and, hiding the halter in one hand, did just what Mom had done. Within ten minutes, the pony had come to the gate and was standing with his nose by my shoulder. "Here," Mom said, slipping a small tin into my free hand.

It was a tin of her special powder that she made from herbs and old bits of chestnut – the horny growths on the inside of horses' legs. I had seen her use it with new horses many times. It calmed them down.

Moving slowly so as not to alarm the pony, I eased the lid off the tin and rubbed a little of the gritty grey powder on to my hands, then I held out my palms towards the buckskin. He snuffed at them and then lifting his muzzle to my face, he breathed out. I breathed in his sweet hay-scented horsy breath and breathed out softly. He snorted and lowered his head.

I slowly lifted the halter and fastened it on to his head. All the time his dark eyes watched me but, to my relief, he accepted my touch. I unbolted the gate.

"We're going to take you home now," I said.

"Ask him to come with you, Amy, don't tell him," Mom said quickly. "He's got to feel you respect him. If he feels that, I'm sure he'll do what you want."

"Shall we go to the trailer?" I asked the pony.

He looked at me for a long moment with unblinking dark eyes and then he stepped forward and followed me out of the pen. As we walked up the aisle, I felt people looking at us and nudging each other. Clearly everyone was stunned by the change in him.

Smiling to myself I led the pony out of the barn and over to our trailer. Without hesitating, he followed me up the ramp and inside.

"Well done," Mom said, putting up the ramp and coming round to the jockey door. I looked round and seeing the pride in her eyes, I felt suddenly warm.

"So what are you going to call him?" she asked, as I got out of the trailer.

I thought for a moment and glanced back inside at the buckskin, who was now pulling at a haynet. Suddenly I remembered how, in the barn, the sun had streamed in through a gap in the roof and danced on his golden coat.

"Sundance," I replied.

A must-have companion book
to the *Heartland* series.

Amy's Journal

Share Amy's memories of the people and
horses who inspire her in her own personal
diary. Learn the techniques and remedies
used at Heartland, find out how to read
a horse's character from his face, and take
an exclusive peek at Amy's collection of
newspaper cuttings, notes and favourite
family recipes.

Healing horses, healing hearts. . .